Year of the Cat

The Thirteenth Realm (Part 1)

A Novel

By Kendi Thompson

Author: Kendi Thompson

Copyeditor: Stephanie Marshall Ward

Contributing artwork: Skylar Purvis

ISBN-13: 978-0692581643
ISBN-10: 0692581642

This book is dedicated to those who dare to challenge, believe in the goodness of humanity, and practice the power of love.

Artwork by Skylar Purvis

Prophecy of Balance

"There must be balance," Source repeated,
"For mankind to flourish on the Earth-Throne he's seated."

His life is a gift from the gods, they created,
And the power to wield choice, but the outcome is
weighted.

Seeing the harm and chaos humans manifest,
Wore heavily upon the goodness within their immortal
breast.

But the gods disagreed, and two groups they split,
Each one possessing their own talent and wit.

One side fights for freedom of Man's soul,
But the other wants slavery, and Man to control.

So Source cried, "Enough! Now Observers will be sent,
To assist with human minds you've cleverly bent!"

For balance, the pendulum won't sway too far to one side,
And Universal Laws each god must abide.

The gods agreed, but did not stop with their plan,
To influence mankind as much as they can.

Then the bell rang out that Earth was again unsteady,
So the gods chose the Observer, and announced they were
ready...

One

A low-pitched clicking, from the soles of his black leather boots, echoed on the smooth gray marble floors. Heron boldly entered the great sunlit oval room, surrounded by stained glass windows and a domed skylight. Bright colors shifted, dancing in waves across the translucent walls below.

He stopped short and stood like a statue, unmovable. His gaze lingered on the other members of the Council of Elders sitting around the crystal table. He paused, measuring his words. Only a small ray of sunlight brushed his dark wavy hair and silken cheek, displaying the beauty, strength, and resilience of this immortal god.

Another Elder approached him. *"Welcome, Heron,"* Rhys spoke telepathically. *"Please, sit."*

Eleven sat around the long crystal table, making a total of twelve gods in the room; the thirteenth spot was empty. Nodding out of respect, Heron pulled back his chair to join them.

Not a single word formed in their immortal mouths, but Heron's frown spoke volumes. After the Council had conspired behind his back, why wouldn't he fiercely advocate for his Charge?

"We understand you have some concerns?" Rhys asked.

Heron let out a long breath. *"Whose clever idea was this?"*

The Council members gawked at one another, sensing the wrath boiling. They were all privy to the charade and didn't look forward to facing him. They must tread lightly.

Heron waited for a response before proceeding. *"This is not part of her chart. It is too dangerous. She is not prepared..."*

"She is prepared," interrupted Brogan, the Council Leader. *"There is no doubt she is capable."*

"No, she is not!" Heron barked aloud, breaking their psychic bond. "You must choose someone else!" He slammed the Life Chart on the table and pointed at it. "Show me here, anywhere on here, where it states she is to do this!"

Brogan stood up. "I understand your duty to protect her, but we cannot ignore the imbalance anymore. You are aware of the situation, no?"

Heron clenched his jaw, waving the parchment before them. "Since when does a Life Chart change without consulting the Advisor first?"

"We had to do it this way. Would you be willing to risk the fate of the Universe and humanity on another who is less capable... let alone explain why you intervened?"

Heron rose to his feet, glaring at Brogan. "I am not only her Advisor, but an Elder of this Council as well. Who decided to leave me out of the final plans?"

"She did," he replied, approaching Heron. Brogan pulled a small rolled piece of parchment from his inner shirt pocket and poked Heron's broad chest with it. "Here is the revision."

Heron hesitantly grasped the scroll and unfolded it with trembling hands. The amendment had taken a surprising turn, far from what he had agreed to. The smack of betrayal stung his face. Trying to restrain himself, he looked at Brogan. "How am I supposed to do this? I can only advise her so much through the veil." Surely he understood Heron's predicament.

"You will not work through the veil. She will come to us."

"How?" he asked, confused.

"Like those before, she will stand in this room," replied Maeve, a female Elder.

"Are you out of your mind!? How will she complete this without becoming conscious of her true nature?"

Maeve smiled. "She will not be aware... not until the end."

Heron pondered her words. This monumental task could easily go awry, choking off any hope of achieving their original goal. Even an immortal god would doubt his ability to pull it off without dire consequences. He sat back down, shaking his head.

"Do not worry, this is all planned." Brogan patted him on the shoulder. "It is her time to do what she agreed to; have faith. We cannot stand in the way, and neither should you."

Heron's voice sliced through the room. "It is not about standing in anyone's way. It is about keeping her safe in the process! She is my Charge... my responsibility. What will happen when the Brotherhood finds out? Did you consider the consequences?"

Maeve leaned over and touched his arm. "We are taking every precaution to ensure that they do not."

"And if they do?"

"Procedures are in place."

"What procedures?" Heron sat down. "How do you plan to do this?"

Brogan turned his back to Heron and walked around the table. "She will meet both groups and report."

Heron began to speak but hesitated, shaking his head in disbelief. There had to be a bigger agenda in motion. What the Council planned seemed careless. Something was not right. Didn't they believe he was savvy enough to catch on?

"This is too complicated, despite what you may all believe. The Brotherhood will find out and do horrible things. When they do, will you allow events to unfold and do nothing?"

Brogan spun around. "No, we will not. That is why we are

going to switch out the normal protocol during the Questioning."

"What do you have planned?"

"We will be preparing her for the worst. Specific methods will be utilized that are not normally practiced," continued Brogan. "I hate to betray her trust, but even you can see the reasoning."

"I am comforted in knowing I am not the only one being betrayed." Heron fiddled with the scroll. "I am to stand by idly?"

"You will not be able to play her devoted Advisor during the Questioning," Brogan replied. "You must make her stand on her own, it is critical."

Heron slammed his fists on the table. "I cannot do that!"

"You are caught off guard, and I am sorry," Brogan said calmly, returning to his seat.

"We are not immune to the Brotherhood's tactics, and you understand as well as I that they will do everything in their power to manipulate her. Once they succeed, what is your failsafe plan?"

Brogan grimaced. "That thought is one we will not entertain. They always hide their own in the shadows... the game is never fair in the first place. Measures must be taken."

Heron grabbed the revised Life Chart. "I am glad someone is comfortable with those measures, because they sure as hell are not listed anywhere on here! And I doubt she would have agreed to any of this if she had understood the stakes were this high!"

"We are gods." Brogan smiled and waved his hands. "We can influence. She is strong and can endure. I would not want anyone else in this position."

Heron glanced at each Elder. "Are we forgetting what she is

capable of? Do not pretend. I can sense the unease among you."

"What would you propose in such dire circumstances?" Maeve asked.

The weight of her words settled upon him. "This is insane. We are going to condemn her."

"It is to her advantage, and ours, that she not remember," Brogan replied.

"Heron, please understand the plan is in motion. We cannot argue this any further. You must retrieve her now," Maeve said.

Heron stood up, taking in a long, deep, cleansing breath. "What if she fails?"

The entire Council of Elders looked at him stoically, getting up from their seats. They exited the room one by one.

"I cannot protect her!" Heron cried.

The Elders ignored him.

Soon the crystal table was void of all the gods but one. If Heron had known about this plan, he could have petitioned Source for another way, but it appeared he had no say in the matter.

He sat, staring off into the distance. The complete silence sent chills up his spine. Prisms of light bounced off the walls around him while he ran his hands through his dark hair, considering other options. He couldn't believe what he was about to do.

The plan was in motion, and he must go to her. Heron groaned, kicking his chair away from the table. He spun around and stormed out.

Two

Machines hissed behind the counter where a redheaded barista prepared a latte or some specialty drink. The manager, a young, pretty thing, barked instructions at a newbie taking orders at the drive-thru window. The other baristas huddled together, discussing their latest Facebook "Likes" and the risky selfie one of them had taken in the bathroom earlier.

Between the jazz music blaring over the speakers, a heavy coffee aroma flooding the air, and bright trendy décor on the walls, the ambiance offered no peace to those who just wanted to relax.

A woman's laughter, while she chatted on her cell phone, added to the sensory overload. Her annoying cackle vibrated through the room, piercing it like a knife splitting the air.

Catriona Blair sat in the corner, her hands wrapped around the warm coffee mug, eyes closed. If it weren't for the irritating woman, she could have dozed off at the round wooden table despite the activity around her. The frigid early February weather and exhausting week had taken its toll. Cat wanted to decompress with a soothing mocha latte before going home to take care of the endless chores awaiting her.

The café sat empty, except for a few souls lingering that dreary Friday evening. She looked around, heavy-eyed. A twenty-year-old hipster, with long black hair pulled into a messy ponytail, sat with his back to her, staring at his iPad. He kept fidgeting with his earphones and swiping the screen like he was swatting a bug.

Cat's cell phone beeped, refusing to be ignored in the overstuffed "Mom" purse. The thought of being reached at any given second annoyed her. She checked the text message and replied to her husband, confirming their evening plans. *No, I won't be going, but enjoy yourselves.* She laid the phone on the table; it read 5:14 p.m. Cat sighed. She'd be horrible company.

The woman cackled again, evoking a dirty look from Cat who picked up her latte and took another thoughtful sip. Cat's indigo eyes shifted from the ponytailed man to the baristas and back to the laughing hyena. The café seemed surreal. Catriona didn't want to go home. She wanted to be in solitude to ponder, but with the cold, rainy weather, no other place was within walking distance except the café, which sat only a few blocks away from where she worked.

Putting her hands to her head, she took in a deep breath. *Get a grip on yourself, Cat. There's no logical reason for feeling like this.* Lacking energy and preferring sleep had become her normal routine. She was definitely in a funk. Maybe the crappy winter weather was to blame.

"Damn!" she moaned.

An impending shadow hovered over her 24/7, and reality seemed like a video, on a loop, played over and over again. She was lost, and this wasn't what she had envisioned for herself at thirty-six years of age, but Cat had always been different.

Her unusual journey had begun the day of her birth, when she came into the world with the Seventh Veil, a thin membrane covering her face. Mystics suggest it signifies a child with special abilities. Her mother, a hippie, into all kinds of natural, organic things, took this as a sacred sign. She chose an Irish/Scottish Gaelic name, Catriona, pronounced (ka-TREE-na), which means "pure."

Blessed with the gifts of sight and healing, Catriona became good at reading people. Her visions could predict outcomes efficiently, which had always seemed natural to her but odd to others. Although these abilities benefited those around her, they became both a blessing and a curse. Some people shunned her, and others embraced her. Catriona became the helpless-helper, able to "see" for others but not herself. She often laughed at the irony.

With these gifts, Cat never seemed to fit in, no matter how hard she tried, only confiding in her family and close friends. If she'd been living in the Middle Ages, she would have been labeled a witch. Luckily, the twenty-first century had shaken up society, allowing differences to be tolerated and old ways questioned and examined. Even today, however, it was funny how quick people were to fear those who are different.

Growing up a happy child, especially in her room, she had preferred solitude. Simple things, like watching the birds in her mother's feeder, which hung underneath the huge maple tree outside her bedroom window, made her smile. At one time, she had identified every species of bird. Her compassion for every living creature, even the ugliest bugs and spiders, didn't go unnoticed. At first, Cat was taught to kill the bugs, but she soon began trapping the creepy crawlers before setting them free outside, unharmed.

Nature mesmerized her, piquing her curiosity. Getting up close to examine the bees pollinating the big purple irises lining the back wall of her brick house intrigued the little girl. She'd often start talking to them. But certain memories, specifically ones from her childhood, wouldn't surface, as if sections had been erased.

As she got older, her talents waxed and waned, and her differences became more noticeable. Cat didn't think or act like others, so she kept tighter reins on her behavior. Sometimes people labeled her a snob, but having to explain herself had become too complicated. Keeping people at a distance was much easier.

Her insights on various topics intrigued her friends, so much so that, during her teenage years, she took on a counselor role. They sought out Cat's advice for all their problems. But internalizing other people's pain made it hard to separate their feelings from her own. Often she became ill, which forced her to seek out a better way to protect herself from the energy of others. A career studying behavior and the human brain looked like a good place to start.

After graduating with a master's degree in psychology, Catriona counseled children at the local clinic. Her ability to clarify things for children stemmed from a strong desire to impart her knowledge, especially about things she had not understood at specific stages of her own childhood.

Later, in her twenties, she met Adam, who worked at the city hospital as an anesthesiologist. They met when Catriona underwent a gall bladder operation. Her outpatient surgery ended up being a three-day stay for observation due to an allergic reaction to the anesthesia, which she playfully blamed on Adam to this day. His adorable smile and horrible jokes greeted her daily while he stood by her bedside. Cat laughed only because of his endearing nature and ridiculous humor, but the six-year gap in age made him attractive – he was an older, presumably grounded, man.

Eventually, Adam got up the nerve to ask for her phone number. They dated for eight months before marrying and settling into the house he'd shared with his previous wife. The details of the divorce had been amicable, but moving in proved uncomfortable at first. Awkward remnants of the previous marriage required a complete overhaul of the decorating to give everything a fresh new start.

About a year later came a daughter, Chelsey, soon to be followed by Cat's younger daughter, Caitlyn. The girls displayed an easygoing nature, full of wonder and exploration. They were a treat to be around, free spirits enjoying the simple things, a quality she hoped they'd never lose. Often they imitated their mother's healing abilities by laying hands on each other when one of them fell ill. Cat enjoyed showing them the proper hand positions and working in the kitchen to make herbal concoctions, hoping they might cultivate the same skills.

Cat took another sip of her latte, wondering why her abilities had disappeared, replaced by a lightheaded, disconnected feeling, like a bubble floating around. It was such a strange sensation. One minute she was floating, and the next she was shoved back into her body. This phenomenon happened randomly and could go on for several minutes. At first, Cat thought maybe a trip to the doctor was in order. Sometimes she'd get a ringing in her ears, but she wrote it off as allergies.

The thought of middle age sickened her. Why must one go through the uncomfortable transition from the Maiden to the Mother... and, after that, the Crone? This deterioration of the body and mind, which was to follow, seemed a cruel fact of life and one she refused to accept gracefully.

"I'll show you middle age," she blurted out.

The twenty-year-old turned around to stare at her.

Catriona ignored him.

Recalling the latest girls' night, when she had returned home with a tattoo, made her smile. It stood as a reminder about choice. After drinking four vodka martinis and enduring three hours with a wicked needle, Cat had her permanent marking. Often, she'd spy the large sexy Siamese cat inked on her right shoulder blade when getting out of the shower. Reflected in the mirror through the warm mist, this symbol of an agile, graceful animal reminded her of the woman she wanted to be. A woman in control of something.

Cat looked out the window, wrapping her long brunette hair around her finger, a habit she'd had since she was a kid. Mulling over certain intervals in her life, she had concluded that anticipating one thing but experiencing something totally different seemed to be the norm. While reminiscing over her youth, a mysterious memory resurfaced.

One evening when she was nine years old, she danced in the grass under a huge harvest moon in her backyard, peering up into the heavens dotted with a million stars and planets. It gave her little soul so much hope, like a celebration that she was part of. Although it was well past her bedtime, she wanted to keep dancing under the October moon as the cool autumn breeze blew across her skin in her white cotton nightgown.

When she looked up into the star-filled sky, her consciousness zoomed into oneness with the universe. All of her fears disappeared, giving her a sense of belonging and security in a world she seemed so separate from. But it was only a fleeting moment, and soon her mother called her to bed. What confused her the most was what happened afterwards.

She awoke the next morning to discover dried leaves stuck to her feet. Throwing back the covers, she grabbed a burnt orange colored leaf, scrunching it between her fingers in disbelief. She hadn't been back outside that evening, so how did it get there? That memory had continued to haunt her.

As an adult, her carefree nature vanished. It saddened her to think how easily joy could be crushed under the weight of the routines and obligations of daily life. One's awareness of the miracles of existence is washed away unless one holds onto it, with bloodied hands, refusing to let go.

Now she sensed a shift, not only in herself, but in society as a whole. People seemed detached from one another, and corruption was blossoming. With her intuitive skills, she had a role to play in all this, but she didn't know what it was. She felt like a racehorse held at the gate just before it opens.

A blast of cold air blew several napkins off the counter as a man opened the café door. Catriona shivered at the assault. She had never liked winter. The Northeast stayed too dark too long. Cat wanted to go home, crawl under her comforter, and hibernate until spring.

The man picked up the napkins and returned them to their rightful place before strolling further into the café. Walking past her table, he paused and turned toward her. Although his face was partially hidden under the hood of his dark coat, a true warmth shone from him. He smiled at her. Cat nodded, cordially smiling back.

As if floating toward Catriona, his arresting blue eyes commanded her attention. The closer he got, the more hypnotic his stare. He pulled her to him like a magnet. The high-pitched ringing began echoing in her ears; then the slow spinning, dizzying feeling overcame her, causing the familiar floating sensation. She viewed herself and the stranger in third person, staring at one another while waves of energy radiated between them. Moments later, Catriona found herself staring at the adjacent wall, painted with coffee cups and slogans.

The cackling woman brought her back to reality.

Gently shaking the cobwebs from her head, she glanced around to see where the man had gone, but the stranger was nowhere to be found. Catriona felt disappointed. She looked down at her phone; it was now 5:46 p.m. Where had the time gone?

Panicked, she took a last gulp of her latte, placed the mug in the plastic bin on her way out, and scurried through the door.

Three

The damp, bitter cold took her breath away the instant she stepped outside. Cat yanked up the hood of her black insulated winter coat. As she strolled down the street in her new leather boots, puffs of misty, warm air trailed from her lips while freezing rain poured in the dark night. How she hated this time of year. The older she got, the more she minded it.

Her Honda sat parked on the other side of the street. People shuffled up and down the sidewalk, bumping into one another, trying to get out of the drizzle. The glow of neon signs and traffic lights reflected on the black pavement, as the water slowly turned to ice.

Catriona glanced both ways before scurrying across, but she stepped in a deep puddle of slush. Shaking off the water, she grumbled as a horn from an oncoming car bellowed, startling her.

"Asshole!" she yelled.

At her car, she rummaged through her purse for keys, but couldn't find them. Cat slammed her purse on the hood. How she couldn't find the twenty-something keys she lugged around all day boggled her mind. Fishing for them, she moaned, wondering if they were on the table in the café, and sprinted back across the street.

When she stepped onto the icy curb, her boot lost traction and she fell on her back. A vision of blinding lights and silver stars rattled around in her skull. A distorted figure converged upon her, causing more disorientation. Blinking several times, she made out the shape of a man hovering above her. The stranger's hand touched her shoulder while he spoke gently. Cat couldn't hear him though, and his face was hidden under his hood.

"Are you OK?" he asked again.

She gingerly sat up and finally recognized the man from the café.

"Yes... I'm fine." She rubbed the back of her head, and her face flushed with embarrassment.

"Here, let me help you." He offered his gloved hand and pulled her to him in his firm grip. Then he inspected her for a second and smiled. "Are you certain you are all right?"

She blinked. "Yes... thank you for your help." Cat looked around wondering why no one else seemed to notice them standing in the street.

"That was a close call. Are you sure you are not hurt?"

"Seriously, I'm fine." She checked herself. "But my boots aren't happy."

The stranger flashed a big smile. "I am sure your boots will forgive you."

"A poor choice to wear leather today, I suppose." Cat shrugged.

A woman with white UGG boots nearly barreled into Cat as if she were invisible, but the stranger snatched her arm and pulled her out of the way.

"Please, come with me," he insisted.

He shuffled her to the side of the curb, holding her hand securely in his, and kept walking. She felt lightheaded again. They had already walked a couple of blocks before it dawned on Cat that she was following a complete stranger.

Digging in her heels, she resisted him.

The man stopped and turned around to face her, but he didn't let go. Dressed in a long black trench coat, beaded with frozen rain, he was much taller than Catriona, who was only five feet, four inches in height. Most of his face was blocked by a shadow cast by the lamppost shining directly above them, but she felt his intense gaze upon her.

"Let me go!" She struggled, trying to break away, but he held her fast.

The man was strong, and despite all her writhing, he barely moved an inch.

"I said, let me go!"

The stranger didn't budge, his body still and unmovable. They were hidden in obscurity with not another soul around.

"Relax, Catriona," he said softly, removing his hood.

He tilted his head upwards, revealing most of his visage in the muted light. Their eyes locked. The ringing penetrated her ears, and the lightheadedness began building again. In a split second, everything burst into slow motion.

She stared up at him. Her heartbeat thumped through her head in a deafening pitch, as she watched individual droplets of frozen rain come in slow waves, hitting his broad shoulders. Hot vapor swirled around the man's lips before disappearing into the air. "Catriona," he mouthed.

Her vision narrowed as waves of intense physical exhaustion seized her and sent her body spiraling toward the ground.

The stranger swept her limp form into his protective arms, kissing the top of her forehead and nuzzling her cheek. He turned around and carried her into the dim alley before vanishing into the cold haze.

Her consciousness was being fickle. She was aware, yet

unaware. It was the same sensation she'd had when she awoke from a light twilight sleep after surgery. Cat didn't want to move.

"Are you awake?" said a male voice.

The tall stranger knelt and held her in his arms. His body caressed her like a warm, fluffy blanket swaddling a baby, cared for and protected. She tingled all over, caught in a moment between a dream and reality, responsive to her surroundings, but still stubbornly unwilling to awaken.

He shook her lightly. "Wake up."

Cat's eyelids fluttered open, and she moaned in protest before touching the back of her aching head.

"You are safe, do not be afraid," he said in his low, sensual voice.

When her vision focused, the beautiful sapphire eyes from the café stared back at her. Who was this man?

She couldn't help but smile up at him.

"I'm not afraid," she whispered, reaching out to touch his cheek with her fingers. Was he real? What had happened?

Cat lay in the middle of a warm, well-lit oval room. Colorful stained glass windows encompassed the entire area from floor to ceiling. A domed skylight was directly above them, and sunlight pierced through the glass, causing a spectrum of hues to reflect off the walls and the shiny gray marble floor.

The elegant, pristine room had a royal ambiance. Lifelike statues, in pure gold, guarded the doorways. Small gray marble stands, displaying vases and sculptures, dotted the walls, along with paintings in the most amazing colors. And an unbelievably fresh scent, like a grassy meadow mixed with flowers, light and fragrant, permeated the space around her. Not the stench of car fumes and wet pavement. Catriona couldn't help taking in deep, heavenly breaths, exhaling slowly with each sigh.

"Feel better?" The handsome man helped her to her feet.

Cat had no idea where she was. Her first impression was that they'd ducked into the lobby of a five-star hotel for assistance after she fell. But each object appeared to be glowing, and everything was in order, precise and spotless.

To her left was a large elongated table, constructed of what appeared to be quartz crystal. The sun's rays sliced through it, producing a brilliant rainbow effect, illuminating the entire room. Thirteen tall-backed chairs, made of smooth black stone, sat around the table. A huge silver vase, filled with an arrangement of magenta and purple flowers, graced the center. Maybe that's where the delightful fragrance came from.

The stranger helped her take off the wet coat and laid it over one of the chairs before removing his own. He walked toward her. Catriona could see him perfectly now. He had short dark, wavy hair, high cheekbones, and flawless medium-toned skin. He possessed Mediterranean traits, with the exception of his eyes, which were his best feature. Beautiful, intense, arresting blue orbs with long lashes, and his endearing smile captivated her. Cat blushed. The man was gorgeous.

Before she could question him, a set of double doors opened to her right. One by one eleven people, wearing shimmering dark clothing, entered the room. Catriona gawked at the prestigious sight before her, finding it impossible to turn away. They were all elegant with perfect, unblemished features, like the man who stood beside her.

The men were dressed in long-sleeved gray button-down shirts accenting their fit, masculine build. Each wore black cargo-style pants. Most were clean shaven with short hair, but some had beards or ponytails. Some had a rustic appearance, and others were more refined, but all were equally handsome, with prominent features.

The women were impeccable in flowing black dresses. The sheer fabric fluttered in the air with each graceful step. The ladies wore various types of silver and gold jewelry. Several wore their tresses up in long braids with glimmering strands of jewels and ribbons twisted through them; others wore their hair in elaborate buns or even down over her shoulders.

They wore inviting smiles on their faces, welcoming her with their gaze. Catriona was mystified at their loveliness, and not one appeared over the age of thirty-five. These people were attractive, and the most amazing common feature was their mesmerizing eyes. Cat felt like the ugly duckling with her drawn, winter-pale complexion. Here stood a tired woman, while they epitomized vitality.

The dark-clothed strangers sat around the crystal table while her charming escort motioned for her to join them. She hesitantly pulled out a chair and sat at the end while he slipped into the chair beside her. She noticed how they represented different nationalities. Their skin colors ranged from dark to light. She sensed an immediate connection of mutual love and admiration, and for some odd reason it made her cry.

They paused, giving her time to collect herself, realizing how overwhelmed she must be.

One of the women, who had gorgeous black hair and green eyes, leaned over and rubbed Cat's arm.

"You are all right," she said, in a soothing manner.

Catriona continued sobbing and peeked at them through the slits between her fingers, which covered her face. She didn't understand her reaction to their presence, but it couldn't be helped. Embarrassed, she wiped her cheek with the back of her sleeve and sat up, adjusting herself in the chair.

"Welcome, Catriona," said an amber-haired man with fair skin and a goatee. He sat at the head of the table. "We are so glad to see you."

The sound coming from his throat was unlike anything she'd ever heard before. His voice chimed like a musical instrument, smooth and gentle with all sorts of tones, pitches and vibrations. The delightful sound and his charismatic presence resonated throughout the room. It was clear he was the leader, sitting there looking at Catriona with gentle brown eyes that captured hers.

She froze, awestruck, stunned by him... stunned by all of them. The magnificent colors, scents and sounds bombarded her senses, making it difficult for her brain to register anything.

They sat in patient silence, watching the tears continue to pour down her face. Their sympathetic reaction hinted at deep compassion. After several minutes, however, worry crossed their faces and they leaned toward each other mumbling.

Cat finally composed herself. "Where am I?"

They sat back, visibly relieved.

"You are safe here with us," said the amber-haired man with the melodic voice.

She glanced around. "Am I in a hospital?"

"No." He shook his head.

"I don't know why I'm here." She choked, wiping a tear from her puffy cheeks.

"You are in the Thirteenth Realm, and we are the Council of Elders."

Cat blinked at him. "Am I dead?"

A male Elder with ginger hair and twinkling hazel eyes, spoke up. "Well... in a way, but not quite."

"Do not confuse her." scolded one of the female Elders. "Now is not the time to tease."

The dark-haired stranger beside her winked. "No, Catriona. You are alive, from where we are sitting."

Her raw relief and despair jumbled together. "I must be hallucinating?"

"I do understand your confusion, but it is true," he responded.

"How can I be in a Thirteenth Realm, wherever this is... if I'm not dead? Is this Heaven?"

The stranger's fingers stroked her hair lightly with a soothing touch. She had an odd connection to him, but how was that possible with someone she'd just met?

"You are not dead, but if this is what you envision as Heaven, then let it be so."

Catriona inhaled sharply. "Why am I here?"

The man hugged her, speaking softly against her head. "You have been brought here for a purpose."

The words *"you are safe"* kept resonating in her mind. She broke his embrace and glared at him.

"What kind of purpose?"

The amber-haired leader stood. "I am Brogan, the Council Leader. To your right is Maeve, and next to her is Rhys, Cryda, Flann, Kennis, Simon, Lir, Chamberlin, Morgan and Dorrell. And…" He pointed to the handsome stranger. "The gentleman to your left is Heron."

"How did I get here?"

Heron smiled. "I was sent to get you--"

"We did not intend to overwhelm you, Catriona," Brogan interrupted in a honey-smooth voice. "The Elders wanted to make sure you were all right."

Abruptly, the Elders stood in unison around the table and bowed their heads in a graceful manner before exiting the room.

Catriona watched them until all that remained were Brogan and Heron. Maeve glanced back before the door closed behind her. Concern showed on her face, producing a kindred spark between the two women.

Brogan sat back down. "Catriona, you are here with us because you are special. You are what we call an Observer."

Cat was dumbfounded. It was too much to comprehend.

"Do you understand what I am saying?" He waited for a response.

A prickling pain wavered up her spine, and fear gripped her.

She rose to her feet and began to retreat. "This is some sort of a prank. What the hell is going on?"

"No, this is not a prank," Brogan replied.

"I need to leave!" she shrieked. She ran to the door and clawed at it. For some reason it wouldn't open.

"There is nowhere for you to go."

She spun around, panicked. "I have to get out of here. Where is my family? Where are my girls?!"

Heron strode over to Cat and grabbed her firmly by the shoulders, looking at her with the same intensity he had used on the street. Speaking in a soothing, hypnotic voice, he calmed her, making her susceptible to suggestion.

"Your family is well, I assure you. Do not be afraid, Catriona."

He turned around and glared at the Council Leader.

Brogan sighed. "This is a unique state of affairs. Normally, an Observer remembers who they are when they transition over, but this is different altogether... something we have not done before. We need to be more careful."

"Do you think?" Heron snapped.

Brogan cleared his throat. "Please sit down, Catriona."

She mindlessly conceded as Heron escorted her back to her chair. Cat sat down, put her head in her hands, and focused on breathing.

"You are special, Catriona," the Council Leader repeated.

"Yes, you keep saying that... which means nothing," she said.

"I understand why you feel alone and different, always

sensing a higher purpose for your existence on Earth." Brogan folded his hands on the table. "From the time you were a child, you have used your gifts wisely to assist humanity, and we want to offer our gratitude."

Cat continued looking down. "You brought me here to thank me?"

He stood. "I do not want to confuse you any further, but understand all will be explained in good time. For now, acclimate yourself to your new surroundings... get comfortable. Heron will be guiding you. You may ask him anything... within reason."

Catriona glanced over at Heron, who looked stunned.

Brogan strolled regally toward the heavy white doors and opened them with ease before turning around to look at the pair. He bestowed a smile upon them and disappeared.

Four

Heron watched Brogan exit through the doors. Sitting in silence, puzzled, he thought maybe it was some sort of hoax. Any moment the Council Leader would reappear, testing him.

Running his hand through his dark wavy hair, Heron looked at the doors again, then back at Cat, who was staring straight through him.

"Uh, I am not sure where to start," he mumbled.

She continued crying.

Her distress broke his heart. Heron clutched her hand and held it gently. "Please do not cry."

Cat attempted to smile despite her swollen eyes.

This entire arrangement angered Heron to the core. Whatever advantage he could give to his Charge, he'd offer without hesitation. Now that he'd thought about it, Heron had a logical idea; at least, it seemed logical, but over time he'd probably regret it.

He shifted in his seat and tenderly held her face in his hands. "Everything will be all right."

Peering at Cat with his soul-searching gaze, Heron smiled, and a relaxed sigh escaped her lips. The hypnotic pull of his gaze made looking away impossible. A blinding flash of light seared through her brain. Cat flinched, pulling her head to the side. It wasn't painful, just a weird expanding sensation, as if

Heron had exposed a previously untapped gateway into her psyche. The brightness faded almost as quickly as it had appeared.

"Open your eyes, Catriona."

She didn't move.

"Open your eyes," he whispered.

She turned toward him and opened her eyes.

With his fingertips, Heron wiped away the last remnants of tears from her face. *"Better?"*

Cat nodded, then frowned.

Heron had spoken to her, but his mouth hadn't moved. She scanned the room to see who else was around, and put her hands over her ears.

"Yes, I am speaking to you. Are you all right?"

She touched his lips. "How are you doing that?"

"Focus," he commanded.

Somehow they were communicating telepathically. She blinked at him, leaning closer in an attempt to respond.

"Focus on what?"

"Speaking with your mind."

"Oh, OK," she replied in thought.

"Good," Heron smiled. *"We can communicate this way when we are not in the presence of others, do you understand?"*

"This is too weird. How... how are we doing this?"

"This is called 'thought transference.' A more efficient way to converse." Heron stood and scooted his chair in before offering his hand to her. *"Shall we take a walk?"*

Catriona reluctantly accepted it. *"I need a minute to adapt."*

Heron laughed. *"I understand. Do not worry, you will get used to it."*

"I'm dreaming?"

"No, you are awake," he assured her.

Of course she was dreaming. All of this was a dream. She had to rationalize it that way for fear of going mad. Resigning herself to the strangeness, she followed Heron out of the Oval Room.

His boots clicked and hers squished on the shiny floors while they wandered through long hallways made of iridescent pearl stone, marble columns, and more stained glass windows. Gold and silver décor accented the walls, but overall it wasn't decorated lavishly; the true beauty was the design itself. The structure combined different types of architecture, classic Grecian design with a unique Mediterranean flair.

Cat felt like she was ten years old again. *Please don't wake up.* The dream was so detailed. She pretended to be a princess, twirling and giggling while strolling about touching the cool, smooth columns. Sunlight poured through the domed skylight in every direction.

"It's magical." She breathed in the pure, unadulterated air.

Heron chuckled but said nothing. Occasionally, he stopped while she examined something. He didn't seem to be in a rush, but he kept moving.

Eventually, the corridors led to the doorway of a sanctuary. As they entered, it took Cat's breath away. A large cathedral ceiling was supported by pillars made of brilliant clear quartz crystal. Rough multicolored panes glistened in the humungous windows, but upon closer inspection they weren't glass at all, but crystals. In fact, the entire sanctuary appeared to be made of crystals, stone, and marble. The colorful gemstones shone like glass and seemed to be magnified within the sanctuary. She'd never seen anything like it before; it was almost new age and enchanting.

The floor descended into circular platforms going all the way around the room. As they approached the center of the sanctuary, she saw a set of aisle steps on either side.

She peered up in reverence. *"Is this a church?"*

"No, this is the Cathedral, part of the building called the Elder Temple. It is a common area for fellowship. There are no churches in this Realm."

They descended the long stairs.

"But it's like a church, except no pews. Where does everyone sit?"

"Everyone is equal. Unlike on Earth, where people prefer seating arrangements as a declaration of their higher status, there is no pride here. We all commune in a circle on the platforms."

Catriona's eyes scanned the room, captivated. *"What about the altar? Where do the religious leaders stand?"*

The immortal raised his hands to the sky. *They stand right here, in the center for all to see, but we have no ministers or priests."*

"Where do people go to worship?"

"No religion is taught here. Religion is an illusion, a man-made fabrication for the masses, I am afraid."

"What are you?"

"I am a god."

She laughed. *"A god who doesn't want to be worshiped? That's a novelty."*

"True gods do not ask to be worshiped. They want humanity to evolve into their true potential. I have no desire to be worshiped," Heron replied, without a hint of humor.

"So, I'm in Heaven... you said I wasn't dead."

"You are not."

She sat down abruptly. *"I don't understand. How am I able to do all of this if I'm not dead? I'm certainly not on Earth?"*

"Correct."

Catriona shook her head. *"Why would a god want to talk to me? Wait a minute, there is only one God."*

"You believe there is but a single god?" He smiled. *"All of the Elders are gods, and we can communicate with humans if we choose because you are created in our image."*

She placed her hands on her head. *"Why are you speaking with me, then?"*

"I welcome your presence, and what I am trying to show you is truth."

"So, you're a god who doesn't want to be worshiped, and this is a church without religion." She scanned the Cathedral. *"How did all the varieties of religion come about then?"*

He smirked. *"A valid question, and many religions have sprung up with their perceptions of god, all birthed by various leaders during Earth's evolution. Angry god, forgiving god, jealous god... man's freedom of choice allows them to choose whichever version they wish."*

"But religion came from God," she said aloud.

"No that is not accurate." He also spoke aloud. "Through the ages, those leaders have used their powers to create religious texts in many forms. These texts have been rewritten to benefit whoever the leader was at the time, so they could better influence and control their people."

"I disagree."

"And you may do so, but understand this: never did a benevolent god knowingly create numerous religions to confuse humanity and cause conflict. The goal has always been to unite, not separate."

Catriona paused, intrigued. "Yes, I suppose it makes sense."

He walked over to a platform and sat beside her. "Religion has birthed so much corruption. Have you ever wondered why Earth suffers so much? Men judge one another instead of recognizing similarities. In reality, you are all equal."

"I wish it were that way," she replied.

"People are manipulated into believing they must conform to a particular belief, or be condemned. Yet the men who created these rules of "sin" stand in the shadows doing the things they preach against. To make matters worse, one religion will claim they are the only true religion, and all others are false, condemning everyone else to burn in an imaginary pit of burning sulfur."

"You mean Hell," she corrected.

Heron held out his hand and cupped her chin. "Hell is not real, and religion is the foulest form of mind control."

"That's ridiculous. I guess you'll tell me a person cannot be spiritual either."

"No, spirituality is a self-awareness connecting a soul to all creation, a relationship with ALL... and ALL is god."

"Then who is God?"

"Surprise... you found me. Now what do you want to do?"

Cat rolled her eyes. "I'm glad you have a sense of humor, but it's not helping right now."

Her Advisor gave her a joyful smile. "In all seriousness, one should not focus on finding god, rather focus on discovering who you are, and your relationship to everything around you."

With that remark, Heron stood and gently took her arm. "Let us go outside. We have more to explore, but please speak aloud when out in public. We do not want your ability to be noticed."

He escorted her out of the Cathedral.

When they walked through the huge doors to the outside, Cat paused, astonished, at the image before her. The land took on a clarity unlike anything she'd ever seen, like stepping into an oil painting magnified with rich, vibrant tints and hues. Cat had no words. The scenery surrounding them could only be compared to springtime in a park. The light, pure air had an underlying scent of wild flowers, and the temperature felt a balmy 75 degrees.

Everything appeared immaculate. No dried up flower on a stem, no crumpled leaf on the ground, not even a brown blade of grass. Nothing was out of place. Even the pavement shone like sea glass.

Cat forgot about her wet, dirty boots. She looked at Heron, worried.

"You are all right. The boots are clean."

When she glanced down again, they appeared brand new.

Walking down the steps of the Elder Temple, Catriona sensed a communal energy within the Thirteenth Realm. All elements had a purpose and a respect for one another. She sensed no anger, no fear, and no sadness.

Delighted to see people around her representing every race, she noticed they all wore the same styles of clothing in a variety of colors. Heron explained that, during the day, each person wore the color associated with their line of work.

"We have architects, scientists, doctors, philosophers... all kinds of professions. We also have janitors, receptionists, and what you call "blue collar" positions... like on Earth. Each position is equally important."

"Are you saying people actually work here?"

Heron grinned. "Yes, of course they do. Except here, everyone understands their importance and joyfully contributes their talents. It is gratifying both for them and others. What else would they be doing in an afterlife?"

"You said I wasn't dead."

Heron frowned, refusing to say it to her again.

"Do they have to work?" she asked.

"No, but when they enter the Thirteenth Realm, they either already possess or discover talents they wish to share with the rest of society, and they are happy to do so."

Strolling about, they eventually came into an area comparable to a large city. Although she had seen the buildings from a distance, Catriona gasped at their enormity. Some structures appeared ancient, in what appeared to be Roman, Greek and Mediterranean design, and others had an Asian scheme. One building, further in the distance, resembled an Egyptian pyramid. All kinds of architecture were present, some more current and a few looking like something out of a science fiction movie. Each building was at least five times bigger than any found on Earth, and according to Heron, each served a specific purpose.

As the pair walked past enormous buildings of various designs, a passenger monorail zoomed high above them.

"Even though things are similar, this place is more spectacular than anything on Earth," said Catriona, giggling at the people waving at her.

"As above, so below," Heron responded.

She crinkled her face, wondering what he meant by that.

A stretch of buildings, including skyscrapers, restaurants, and condos, lined an enormous body of pure water with boats and ships sailing in the distance. A light breeze blew past, prompting Cat to take in a deep breath and sigh. "I imagined Heaven being full of extremely happy people, running around playing harps and drinking red wine."

"No, you are wrong. The angels do that. And of course, as gods, we all sit on puffy white clouds looking down."

Cat's mouth gaped open. "Are you serious?"

"Of course not!" He chuckled. "Did I not say 'as above, so below'?"

She playfully punched his arm. "Yes, but I hadn't thought about it literally. All right, Heron the 'god,' please share more of your infinite wisdom."

He smiled. "Are you certain you are ready?"

"Yes, if you don't get too technical."

Heron began explaining how Earth was meant to be a miniature duplicate of the Thirteenth Realm. Some structures she'd seen hadn't been built yet, but they would evolve in Earth's future. At one time, the landscape had been the same, but now, after eons of abuse and pollution, the planet paled in comparison.

"Here is paradise, there is not. The Earth could be a paradise if only humans took care of her... and one another. If they did, Earth would have no pollution, no war, and no disease."

"I always wondered what a paradise would be like. Strange thing is I've never felt like I belonged anyway."

Heron didn't respond. Maybe he thought it was unwise to discuss too much with her. He grabbed her hand and squeezed lightly. "Come on, I have somewhere else to show you."

They walked effortlessly out of the big city and crossed a field that went on for as far as the eye could see, until they came upon a wide hill.

"Ready?" he asked.

Normally, Cat would have been out of breath from all the walking, but the pure, fresh air invigorated her body, which gave no hint of exhaustion. How they had managed to walk all the way from the Elder Temple, through the massive city, and now to this hill baffled her. It appeared Heron could take them wherever he wished within a split second, giving the impression they were transitioning from one area to the other seamlessly.

Following him up the huge hill, she admired the grass. The soft green lushness made her crave taking off her boots, so she could squish it between her toes. This is what she loved, being with nature, and the long winter had been harsh.

"Ah." She dropped to the ground to roll around in it. "Dear god, this is what I needed." She plucked a blade of grass to inspect it.

"You are welcome," Heron said, under his breath. He adored her childlike curiosity. "I hate to intrude on your fun," he interrupted, "but we must be going. There is much more to show you."

Cat bounced to her feet and trailed him until they finally reached the top of the hill. She gasped at the breathtaking beauty before her. Off in the distance, massive mountains stretched for miles in every direction, displaying rich shades of blue and purple with such grandeur, it nearly brought her to her knees. The tops reached so far into the clear cobalt sky they couldn't be seen.

How big is the Thirteenth Realm? Breathing in the cooler air emanating from the majestic peaks, Cat noticed something sparkling below the base of the mountain. The sun bounced off three tiny objects.

"What is that?"

Her Advisor held out his hand to her. "Come with me, and I will show you."

Five

They hiked, for what seemed like hours, toward the shiny things. When they got closer, she could make out three tall spires positioned in a triangle formation. Each one was the same height and width as the others. The towers appeared to be made of dark blue crystal emitting a rainbow spectrum of light in every direction. Large trees, bushes, and flowers were elegantly landscaped around each one, and a colossal water fountain, with a reflecting pool made of gray stone, rested in the center.

The blue crystal was unlike anything Catriona had ever seen. The towers were darker at the bottom, becoming more translucent at the top in an ombre effect. A force radiated off of them producing a hypnotic vibration, a happy, calm, peaceful energy. An energy she seemed strangely familiar with. Cat peered up at them, speechless.

Heron looked around and connected with her through telepathy.

"These are the Blue Crystal Towers. They are beacons providing much needed energy to the Thirteenth Realm. Here also, healings are performed for all types of species, including souls who crossed over. I brought you here to show you where our healers work."

"Crossed over from where?" she asked.

"From Earth and other planets. Sometimes when a soul has had a violent death or many difficult and traumatic life experiences, they must come here to rebalance before being reintroduced into our society.

They are cocooned, for a period of time, to heal."

Cat meandered around the towers. *"Does everyone come to the Thirteenth Realm?"*

"Not all, they can choose other dimensions. But those beings who lived an extremely difficult life, or experienced a traumatic death, always come here. Some souls never adapt well to Earth, or other planets."

Her hand pulsed when she touched the tower's smooth, velvety surface. *"I've had dreams about these towers. I've seen them before."*

Cat felt a strong pull. She began walking toward the entrance, but Heron grabbed her arm.

"No, you cannot go in."

That hurt; it felt as if she were being denied access to a place she rightfully belonged. *"Why not?"*

"The energies would be too much for you. In fact, I am sorry to say you cannot enter ANY buildings in this Realm, not until your body is fully acclimated."

"I've been in the Oval Room and the Cathedral with you--."

"Yes," Heron interrupted, *"but that was under special circumstances."*

"How so?"

"You are only touring today. After this, you will be spending your time at the Elder Temple."

She blinked at him. *"I'm a prisoner?"*

Her Advisor reached out and stroked her hair. *"No, Catriona. You are not. But until you finish your mission, we cannot risk you seeing too much."*

Cat cocked her head. She sensed that he wasn't telling her everything. Not even close. *"Oh, yes... my mission. I suppose I should wake up now?"*

Pulling her to him, he gazed into her indigo eyes. *"This is not a dream. You are here, and for a specific purpose."*

She touched his face. *"Heron, this is a dream, an illusion. I hit my head pretty hard when I slipped--."*

"No," he said, aloud, shaking her lightly. "You are standing here, with me, right now."

"Impossible!"

"Nothing is impossible."

"But... Oh... I've got to sit down before I faint." She was wavering on her feet.

Heron caught her. "I wish I could tell you."

"I thought Brogan said I could ask you anything."

"Yes, but he also added 'within reason.'"

Fear lumped in her throat. This was too much.

Heron swept her into his arms and walked toward the fountain. "Sit with me, and I will explain."

He carried her to the reflecting pool, and they sat down. "Are you going to be all right?"

She nodded. Cat instinctively trusted Heron, although she couldn't explain why.

"Not only am I an immortal, but I am also your Advisor."

"What does that mean?" she asked, counting her breaths.

Heron paused. He seemed to be weighing his words carefully. "Think of me as your Guide. I have been with you since the day you were born."

She frowned. "You're telling me you're a guardian angel?"

"I am a god, not an angel. I prefer the title 'Advisor'."

Her mouth gaped open. "You're shitting me."

"I am not. I am quite serious."

"Why would a god want to be my Advisor? What... the angels couldn't handle it?"

He grinned. "It is complicated."

Catriona looked down. All logic and sanity had gone out the window. With what her mortal senses had gathered, she had to believe him. Throwing her hands up to hide her face, she groaned. "Did you see *everything*? Shit, I bet you did."

"Your actions are no worse than any others... although you are spirited, and too curious for your own good. You had a couple of close calls."

"Uh, I'm so embarrassed," she whined through her hands.

"Why would you be? Understand we do not judge."

Cat moved a finger over so she could peek at him. "That's a relief."

Heron grinned at her.

"What am I supposed to call you? Advisor Heron?"

"No, just Heron is fine."

Cat put her hands down. "Well, I'm glad we got that out of the way. This will take some getting used to."

"For both of us."

She was in deep thought for several moments, crinkling her face. "I've prayed for guidance a lot throughout my life."

"You are a deep thinker, Catriona... a wonderful quality about you."

"Sometimes, I'd sense this presence and start talking out loud, and immediately I'd get these thoughts in my head, as if someone had answered."

He smiled. "Yes, but the older you got, the less you talked to me."

His comment stung. "I didn't mean to ignore you."

Heron winked at her. "It goes with the job."

Cat couldn't imagine putting a face to a being she had thought was nothing more than a fairy tale told to children for comfort, and yet here he sat.

She touched his shoulder blade. "Nope, I don't feel any wings back here."

The immortal let out a big belly laugh. "Humans, sometimes you are so endearing."

"I remember when I was little, I'd lie in bed praying for things to get better, and sometimes it felt like someone hugged me."

He wrapped his arms around her. "Did it feel like this?"

"Yes," she whispered, recognizing the exact sensation.

Heron let go. "You had a difficult childhood, Catriona. I hugged you all the time."

"I didn't mean to ignore you. As adults it's not impressed upon us. A Guardian Angel—"

"Advisor," he corrected.

"--is like Santa Claus or the Easter Bunny. Adults are expected to handle things on our own, not reach out to an imaginary friend like when we were kids."

He frowned. "You're the kind of woman who takes on more than she can handle, and gets overwhelmed when she does."

"But I have to be smarter, more resilient. I always say 'put your big girl panties on and deal with it, Catriona'."

"You already are a strong soul, even though you smile through your sorrow, believing you must endure it alone. Asking for help is not a sign of weakness."

"Oh, my dear Heron." She shook her head. "Life is hard. I've played the victim plenty of times, and I'm not doing it anymore. Thinking there's a supernatural being whose job it is to fix everything takes away from me handling my own problems."

Cat felt a pang of sympathy for her loyal guide. "When we get older we must find coping mechanisms, and believing in fairy tale beings... is unrealistic."

His sapphire eyes captured hers. He took her hand and

placed it against his heart.

"But we are real. You need to ask for guidance when life is gloomy, and I will show you beauty. I will show you the positive side to an imbalanced world."

"Life's messy, Heron."

"Why suffer when I am ready and waiting to assist you? Needing help is not putting you in the victim role--it is recognizing when you are not strong enough to handle the situation on your own."

"I'm not one of those people who constantly looks for ways to drop a problem into someone else's lap. I'm a survivor."

"Yes, and I am proud of you. But do not carry the weight alone."

Cat withdrew her hand from his. "If you are a god, why do you allow things to get so bad before doing anything about it? Can't you snap your fingers?"

"I would if I could, but humans make choices affecting not only themselves, but others around them. Those choices create a positive or negative impact, and sometimes you are on the receiving end."

"Then keep the person from making the wrong choice in the first place."

"Wrong for whom? Them, or someone else?"

Her Advisor reached for her hand again. "A good outcome for one might turn out to be a bad outcome for another. It is a domino effect, like throwing a pebble in a pond--the water ripples, affecting everything around it. Whatever choice is made will produce ramifications for all parties involved. But you can always counter with your own choices."

"Not until the damage has already been done."

Heron sighed. "Humans possess the power of choice in all of life's decisions. Angels, Guides, whatever you wish to call us, cannot choose a course of action for you. It is Universal Law."

"But you're a god."

"It does not matter. Certain laws even gods must abide by."

She glanced down, realizing they were arguing. "We mortals have to muddle through it, I guess?"

"The Earth would be a much better place if people learned to be compassionate and harmless to themselves and one another. This is one of the reasons you are here."

Cat snorted. "You came to retrieve me during one of my mental rants in the café didn't you? Why?"

"I cannot say."

"You can't, or won't?"

"I cannot, Catriona... not yet."

"So, you are limited."

He caressed her shoulder. "When you are sad, I am sad, and when you are happy, I am happy. I do what I can. I comfort and care for you. I live every experience you do... contrary to your beliefs. I offer guidance without you even realizing it."

They sat in silence, mulling over each other's responses. The immense wisdom in this immortal--who happened to be sitting beside her, even if she didn't completely understand him--was comforting. The conflict must stem from the whole fate-versus-choice battle.

"But if man is a creation of god, why can't gods intervene with their own creations?

"We cannot intervene, only influence. Would you prefer your life fated? If everything were decided for you the day you were born, either good or bad, would it make you happier?"

She shook her head. "No. I want control over my own life."

Heron nodded.

"What you say will hopefully make sense to me someday." Cat ran her fingers through her hair. "I never meant to hurt your feelings."

Her Advisor appeared touched. Maybe a god feels through his creation, not the other way around.

"You never hurt my feelings," he said.

Cat smiled, as a lightbulb went off in her head. "What if I give you permission to make a choice for me, can you do that?"

He seemed amused. "Only under extremely rare circumstances. So rare, in fact, the choice I make would have to also affect me."

"Oh, that sounds too complicated."

"Yes, it is."

Feeling like a child seeking validation, she asked if she had turned out all right.

Leaning over, Heron kissed her cheek. "I am proud of you, Catriona. You are an amazing soul."

His approval meant the world. She threw her arms around him.

Balfour, a god from the Fortress of Shadows and a member of the Brotherhood, hid behind a tree. He'd been following them since they left the Elder Temple.

The minion scratched his head, trying to understand why a Council Elder was escorting the newly arrived Observer around the Thirteenth Realm. The Brotherhood knew she was there, but they were confused as to why her presence had not been made formal.

He turned back toward the Fortress of Shadows located at the far edges of the Realm. It was his duty to let Ruarc know the Observer had arrived.

Six

Cat felt disoriented and had the odd sensation that time was not passing. Physically, her limbs ached and she had a ravenous appetite, but mentally she was overwhelmed. To her, everything seemed eternally *in* the present without any thought of past or future events, as if each precious moment was perfection.

As she and Heron entered the Elder Temple, they found Brogan waiting for them in the foyer.

"Come, I want to take you to your chambers. I am sure you are in need of some food and rest," Brogan said.

While they strolled about, Cat searched the walls for a clock, or some indication of the time of day. She peered up at the skylight, but the sun shone as brightly as it had earlier when Heron took her outside.

"Do you have the time?" she asked.

The amber-haired one turned to her, amused, with a sparkle in his eloquent, melodic voice. "What time do you want it to be?"

She looked at him, confused.

"Let me explain it to you this way," Brogan said:

"Time is an illusion marking the ebb and flow,
Of when to hold on and when to let go.

It marks the seasons to sow and reap,
A rhythm to rise and a rhythm to sleep.

The days and nights go by so fast,
For the mortal flame is not meant to last.

When you stop for a moment to ponder and think,
You discover days disappeared in a wink.

Only when you are old, staring down death's door,
Do you wish for more time like you had before.

But the truth is, a soul returns home to be free,
From the cycle and bondage of time, you see?"

Cat enjoyed the delightful poem. "You're a poet, and don't know it, Brogan."

"I try." He grinned. "Understand, dear Catriona, there is no time in the infinite."

How could anyone live without the knowledge of time? She couldn't wrap her mind around the word "infinite." Time marked everything in life with a beginning and an end. If life is infinite, who developed life, and how can something go on without death, change, or digression? This enigma had plagued Cat since she was a little girl, for the thought of physical death scared her.

"Hmm... I see this is a topic we will need to discuss at greater length." Brogan stroked his short beard.

They escorted her through the long corridors and eventually stopped at a large rustic red wooden door.

"This leads to your chamber. I am sure you will be pleased. We also do not sleep, but I do not want to confuse you with that concept either."

"Please, no more poetry," she said.

He chuckled, opening the door. "Rest here. Food will be provided along with some other essentials you will need. I am sure you are hungry."

"Yes, famished. Do you eat?"

Brogan exchanged another glance with Heron. He probably assumed an interesting conversation had taken place on their tour.

He flashed his pearly white teeth. "We can if we choose, but it is an activity we created primarily for human experience."

"How do you receive nourishment then?" she mumbled, drained by fatigue.

"We are energy, and as such we receive our nourishment from the Source, but again, that is another conversation for another time."

She turned to Heron, who stood behind them. *"Would you care to stay with me?"* she asked telepathically.

He didn't look at her; he appeared to be concentrating on something on the ground.

"You MUST speak when we are around others," he beamed back.

Cat spoke aloud. "Heron. Would you like to stay with me?"

"Thank you, but no," he replied.

Why did she feel rejected? Her Advisor seemed distant all of a sudden.

"I would, but I have other commitments." He still refused to meet her eye.

Cat nodded toward Brogan. "How about you?"

"I would enjoy that, but now there are Elder things to do. I hope you understand."

As the men turned to leave, Cat grabbed Brogan by the arm. "OK, the truth is I don't want to be alone. And you still haven't answered my question. Why am I here?"

Brogan cleared his throat. "All will be explained to you tomorrow."

"I thought you had no concept of time. Tomorrow is future time," she teased.

Brogan's tender brown eyes lingered on her. "Tomorrow gives the impression of things to come. You are tired, and for your well-being, dear Catriona, we will speak with you… Tomorrow."

"OK," she muttered, eyeballing both of them. "After I eat and get some rest, would someone explain what the hell I'm doing here?"

"Yes, I will," Brogan said. "Goodnight, Catriona."

"Goodnight."

He spun around to leave.

Cat listened as the sound of Brogan's footsteps faded at the end of the corridor.

Heron faced her and wrapped his arms around her waist. "Calm down, Catriona. You are all right, I will be down the hall."

She immediately relaxed, looking up into his dazzling sapphire eyes. *You had better be.* Heron broke their embrace and walked away to leave Catriona to her own devices. She watched him disappear through a door halfway down the hall and took a deep breath before opening the red door to her chamber.

Heron waited for her to go into her chamber before sneaking out to catch up with Brogan. He wasn't looking forward to tomorrow. In fact, he dreaded it. Everything would be different. How would he be able to idly stand by during the Questioning? He wanted to kick himself.

When Cat entered the massive chamber, she had no idea

what awaited her. Abruptly stopping in her tracks, she surveyed the spacious room in disbelief. The white walls appeared to shimmer all the way to the high ceiling. To the right was a large wood-framed bed with a sheer, iridescent sage colored canopy. Huge fluffy white pillows and a sage down comforter sprawled across the bed. Catriona stroked the comforter, admiring its softness before taking a nose dive into the pillows.

Rolling around, laughing, on the firm, heavenly mattress, she noticed, on the opposite side of the room, a large fireplace with two-toned tan marble pillars. A roaring fire had awaited her arrival. An enormous silver vase held sweet, fragrant magenta flowers that draped down onto the mantel, neatly covering every square inch of it. In front of the fireplace was a tan Victorian-style sofa, a side table, and a multicolored Tiffany lamp.

Dumbfounded, she strolled over to the large walk-in closet to the far right. A huge crystal chandelier hung from the ceiling, casting a dim light on a long rack of clothing. Catriona thumbed through the garments, stunned by the beautiful designs. A row of pants and even some jeans and shirts were neatly folded in a dresser, facing the clothes rack, and an assortment of shoes lined the wall. A sage velvet settee faced the mirrors on the left wall. A tall jewel-encrusted armoire stood at the back of the closet. Its wooden drawers were filled with earrings, necklaces, and bracelets crafted from silver, gold, and gemstones.

Cat danced with delight. She yanked off her drab winter clothes and clunky boots and threw them onto the floor without a second thought. Then she snatched a purple dress off a wooden hanger. She eagerly put it on and ran to the jewelry armoire to find a matching bracelet and necklace. When she turned to look at herself in the mirror, she realized she hadn't felt this pretty in a long time. Catriona curtseyed at her reflection. Then she twirled around the room to discover more treasures.

She twirled into the lavish bathroom and squealed at the six moveable shower heads up and down the wall. Such luxury. Beside the shower a sunken tub, displaying an assortment of bath salts, shampoos, body oils and lotions, made her ecstatic. She grabbed a bottle with yellow flowers on it and took a long deep whiff. The essence of jasmine filled her nostrils, evoking a blissful moan. One by one Cat opened each bottle, sniffing the heavenly scents. She loved smelly stuff.

Back in the bedroom, a faint glow seeped through long sheer sage curtains to the right of the fireplace. The fabric danced in a light breeze blowing in from somewhere. She gracefully parted them to discover an outside terrace made of glistening white stone. Torches were lit on either side, and two copious full moons peeked out from behind the clouds, bathing her in an opaque light.

The cool, fragrant night air tickled her cheek. She inhaled and sighed at its enchantment. As she gazed at the stars twinkling high above her, a gust of wind blew through the silky purple dress, gently touching her skin. An outline of the majestic mountains offered a sense of protection and peace. This was paradise.

Her moment of tranquility ended with a loud knock on the door. She scurried back into her chambers and opened the red door cautiously. A short man dressed all in white gave her a curt smile while rolling a cart of covered food on a round silver tray. He stopped in front of the fireplace and busied himself by laying out a china plate, cloth napkin, silverware, and a long-stemmed glass of red wine on the side table.

He turned to her. "Enjoy your meal."

"Thank you." Cat watched him leave.

She eagerly sat down and took off the silver lid. She gasped. It was a variety of her favorite foods. At least two dozen clams with drawn butter, green beans with sliced almonds, and cherry tomatoes with fresh basil, mozzarella, olive oil and sea salt. Under another lid were chocolate-covered strawberries and a small slice of cheesecake drizzled with raspberry sauce.

Cat grabbed a fork and sliced off a chunk. *Now this is Heaven.*

When Heron and Brogan returned to the Oval Room, the rest of the Council seemed to be anxiously awaiting their arrival. In addition to preparing for the Questioning, they had disturbing news to share.

Chamberlin lunged toward the two other gods at the door. "Ruarc is aware she is here."

"Fine." Brogan waved his hand. "He cannot get his claws on her until we are done. We always get the Observer first."

"But he sent Balfour to spy and watch her every move."

"And I would expect them to be doing so," Brogan answered. "He is predictable. His minions are everywhere."

Heron had been with Catriona most of the day, and at times they hadn't spoken a word. To an onlooker, spy or not, it must have appeared unusual. He cringed at the thought of their telepathic communication being discovered. Opening thought transference with a mortal was something an immortal wasn't supposed to do, but as Heron saw it, she would need every ounce of help he could give her.

Brogan appeared to study Heron for a moment, before he turned to the other Elders.

"The Questioning will not be pleasant for *anyone* involved. Can we please stay focused? It is a safe assumption Catriona will not be happy either, but we cannot let that hinder our duties. I suggest we all take some time to recharge and be ready first thing."

The other members silently nodded, all except Heron.

"You seem troubled," said Brogan.

Heron gave him a sideways glance. "Why would I not be?"

Brogan grinned. "She will get through this and come out far better than expected. I assure you."

"You cannot assure anything," Heron mumbled. He turned and exited the room.

After all the Council members had left, Heron walked back down the corridor toward the Cathedral. Upon his entrance, the twin moons announced themselves through the translucent clouds with their beams touching every corner of the sanctuary. A mist-like form permeated the air. Heron walked into it sighing deeply, allowing the moons' luminosity to encapsulate him in their divine strength and glory.

He couldn't help Catriona to the degree he'd like, but that wouldn't stop him from putting the odds in her favor. With eyes closed, the powerful god raised his arms high above his head, chanting words only immortals had spoken from the beginning of time. Symbols uniformly presented themselves in golden illumination on the floor, pulsating at a slow hypnotic speed.

He lowered his arms, commanding the symbols to burst into a vibration of such high frequency, the atmosphere of the room turned into a strong swirling wind. The air blew with such force, it lifted the symbols off the ground and dispersed them in every direction as Heron fervently continued his chant. He threw his arms out while gusts of air whipped through them, commanding the images to bleed into every object in the room. His words bestowed a blessing, integrating invisible symbols into the room to protect the one he loved.

The god called out one last word with such passion it brought him to his knees. Wind whirled through the temple, shaking the Cathedral to its core before falling deathly calm. The images disappeared as soon as his eyes fluttered open. Pleased with himself, he gazed upwards into the calm of the night sky.

No one needed to know what he had done. The secret stood between him and the steady gait of the luminous moons.

Glancing behind him one last time, he nodded confidently and strolled up the marble steps.

Catriona couldn't sleep under the soft sage comforter. First she was hot, then she was cold. Her mind wrestled between fantasy and reality. It was time to wake up from her blissful dream. Pinching herself for good measure, she felt the pain, but still didn't recognize anything familiar. *Dear God, I'm not dreaming.*

Somehow being in the presence of the Elders, especially Heron, put her in a tranquil state. A happy, trusting, and peaceful energy surrounded them, rubbing off on Catriona. Now, lying there alone, away from their presence, the calming effects were wearing off, and her mind frantically wandered. She began questioning her sanity.

How did she wind up "here," wherever "here" was? More than anything, she wanted to be home with Adam and the girls. How worried they must be. She'd been delightfully overwhelmed (or distracted) --there hadn't been enough downtime to analyze her situation.

A sickening excitement rose in her chest. Part of her wanted to scream. She threw her comforter off and began pacing around the room, glancing every now and again at the moonlight shining through the sheer curtains, beckoning her to come out. Cat walked outside onto the veranda and stared up at the moons. The fact that there were two confirmed she wasn't on Earth. Taking in slow breaths, she tried talking herself down from a full onset of hysteria.

Unable to contain her fear, she ran to the red door and grasped at the doorknob, but her hands went straight through it. Cat tried again, but it was futile. She stepped back and banged on the thick wood, but no sound came from it, as if she'd been trapped in a bubble. Sharp needles of terror pricked at her skin; she screamed frantically.

Her cries resonated down the hall, and Heron ran to her chamber. He lunged for the door, but stopped short and leaned his forehead against the rustic wood listening to the anguished wailing that tortured him. Every fiber of his being wanted to rush in. It went against his nature to let his Charge suffer like this. He must do something.

He barreled through the entrance and found Catriona balled up on the floor. He scooped the crying woman into his strong, protective arms, offering her comfort. She buried her face in his neck, clinging to him in terror. He sat down on the bed and rocked her back and forth, listening to her choke on her tears. It reminded him of the scared little girl from long ago.

"Shh... it's all right," he spoke gently against her ear.

He kissed her forehead, holding her in his loving arms. After several minutes, his tender embrace consoled her and the weeping subsided. Exhausted, she lay still in his trusting arms, drifting to sleep, unaware of the events yet to unfold.

Seven

Sunlight crept over her face, causing a kaleidoscope of colors to bedazzle her from behind closed eyelids. Catriona stirred from her slumber. The solace of her bed was too good to leave, as she stretched and moaned, fighting off her dreamy head. After a few moments, Cat opened her eyes, stretching her arms to the sky. She sat straight up and surveyed the room, realizing she was not in her own bed. The sage comforter fell to the floor, a testament to a fitful night's sleep.

A knock startled her. Cat got out of bed and cracked open the door a few inches to peer outside. Her handsome Advisor stood on the other side. Relief washed over her.

"Good morning, Catriona. Did you sleep well?"

"No, I swear I was screaming last night."

"Are you certain?" he asked.

"Yeah, I think so. Maybe it was a dream, I'm not sure."

He tilted his head. "Well, as an Advisor, it is my job to assist, and with that said, I have come to retrieve you."

His remark seemed oddly formal. Something was off.

"For what?" Cat asked.

Heron waited. "It would be much easier to talk if I could come in."

Glancing down at the jade silken nightgown clinging to her hourglass form, she was about to protest that she wasn't dressed, but he'd already seen her in all her naked glory since birth--why be shy now?

She threw open the door. "Come in."

He walked past her, followed by the shorter man from the night before, pushing a small cart of food.

Cat scurried behind the door, covering herself with her hands.

"I brought you breakfast." Heron turned around.

Taking the cart from the man, he thanked him before pushing it over to the tan sofa. "Here, come have something to eat."

She peeked around the door. The food looked delectable. After the amazing meal she'd had last night, she couldn't help but anticipate the next one.

Cat sat down, eyeing Heron thoughtfully. "Were you here last night?"

"It is nothing to worry about." He shrugged.

"Well... thank you for coming to my rescue."

Heron nodded.

"No, I mean it. Thank you."

"You are welcome." He handed her a glass of orange juice and watched her take a sip. It was the sweetest orange juice she'd ever tasted. "Good?" he asked.

"Delicious."

Her Advisor grinned.

Cat wondered why he had seemed so nonchalant about what she'd said. Something nagged at her, and she wasn't going to let it go. There were too many questions that needed an explanation. Heron wasn't getting off that easy.

While he prepared her breakfast, Cat contemplated her words. Every once in a while, he'd glance over, acting too blasé.

Something was definitely up.

"Heron?" she asked softly.

"Yes?"

"Why wasn't I able to leave the room last night?"

He hesitated. "What do you mean?"

"I tried to leave, but my hand went straight through the doorknob like I was a ghost."

"Catriona, you were so tired, I am sure you only thought you could not get out." He took the empty glass from her to refill it. "Sometimes things appear to be one thing, but are actually another. Your exhaustion made you hysterical."

She considered his words. "No, I became hysterical after I couldn't turn the knob... or bang on the door--no sound came from it." She twisted her hair around her finger. "I was trapped... it was horrible."

Heron sighed. "I am sure it is your imagination."

"No, it isn't. Why are you pretending you don't know what I'm talking about? Maybe all these goodies in my chamber are nothing more than distractions to keep me from walking around the Elder Temple."

"Maybe," he said.

She cocked her head. "I wandered through the room looking at the clothes, the bed, and all the wonderful scented toiletries in the bathroom... and then I went outside on the terrace and looked up at the moons. There are two of them... which is weird."

He handed her a plate of food. "Yes, I suppose it is unusual to you."

"There was a knock at the door. The same guy who followed you in also brought me dinner last night. I ate, but don't remember going to bed."

"Your interpretation is off, and you are overwhelmed right now."

She set the plate on her lap. "I interpreted everything fine! Why won't you validate my feelings?"

"I am validating your feelings. You were distraught, scared, panicked, what else do you wish me to say?"

"Oh... I don't know, maybe, 'I'm sorry you were trapped in here having a mental breakdown,' then explain why I couldn't get out of this freakin' room in the first place."

"I am sorry you felt trapped."

Cat waited for more explanation, but none came. "This isn't funny, Heron! I *hate* being out of control! What's happening to me?"

He silently beamed a thought toward her. *"You were dreaming,"*

She glanced up, beginning to speak, but didn't.

"It was all a bad dream."

Cat popped a berry into her mouth. "Maybe it was a bad dream."

She sat nibbling away at her food. Heron seemed so sweet and lovable. Never had a male tended to her every need. Her self-reliant nature scared most mortal men, and the role of caretaker fell squarely on her shoulders. But there was a familiarity about Heron, and their relationship had grown more intimate on some level. The longer he stayed in her presence, the stronger their bond.

He looked at her. "So, today will be an interesting day for you."

Cat didn't verbally respond. Instead, she tried to get the telepathy thing going, but it wasn't working.

Her Advisor knelt down. "I must visually connect and invite you into my mind first, before you can use that type of communication."

"I didn't know you turned it off."

"It is not like turning a switch on and off, so to speak. I choose when I want you to hear me and when I do not."

"Isn't that convenient."

His nearness made her heart skip a beat, causing her to glance away. She felt like a little school girl with a crush. The immortal's masculine essence rattled her senses. Heron could say the grass was purple and the ocean was orange, and she'd believe anything when he trapped her in those sapphire eyes.

With a brief flash going off in her head, the telepathic connection started. It was like adjusting the lens on a camera. At first the sensation seemed fuzzy, but when the link completed, everything zoomed into focus.

"There," he said with his mind. *"Do you perceive me?"*

"Yes. Am I coming in loud and clear?"

He smiled. *"Remember, we must actually speak to one another in the presence of others. Do you understand?"*

"How long will it last this time?"

"For as long as I want it to. Now, do you understand?"

"Yes..."

He broke visual contact, stood up, and walked toward the fireplace.

"OK, tell me more about this day you planned for me," she said.

He hesitated. *"The Council will be posing all types of questions. You need only answer as truthfully as possible. If you do what Brogan asks, you should be fine."*

"What do you mean by, 'should be fine'?"

"The key is to answer all of his questions without much emotion attached."

She took another bite. *"Is that what other Observers do?"*

"Yes. Keep your responses concise. Do not go off in another

direction. I know you are prone to do that and…"

His closeness made her flush. Her eyes lingered on his gorgeous form, sparking a deep desire within her. Bold images played out in her imagination of what she'd like to do with him, and her thoughts wandered into naughty places.

He glared at her.

"Ah… holy shit!" Catriona sputtered aloud, covering her face.

Heron turned around and loudly cleared his throat.

Mortified, she silently scolded herself as her face turned hot beneath her hands.

"Please remember I am your Advisor," he reprimanded her, breaking the telepathic bond. "This type of conduct is inappropriate."

"I'm so… so sorry. I didn't mean…" Cat looked down. "You're absolutely right, I don't know what came over me." She wanted to melt between the sofa cushions.

He stooped down in front of her and removed her hands from her face. "Look at me. I'm not judging you, Catriona. You are human, and desire is a human trait, but in order for us to maintain our relationship, you must discipline your thoughts when I am around."

Cat nodded. "I didn't mean to cross that line."

Heron stood. "Finish eating and get dressed." He spun around and exited the room.

She threw her hands up in the air, rolling her eyes, "Oh, Catriona… You idiot."

Heron stood on the opposite side of the chamber door to compose himself. The vision of Catriona's slim, curvy figure, clad in the jade nightgown, was difficult to erase from his mind. It took all his immortal strength not to go back in, sweep her into his arms, and give in to his own desire.

She intuitively picked up on the exact nature of their relationship, making this a sticky, tangled web. Being together was bound to cause this, and he couldn't blame her, considering their history, although she had yet to be made privy to it. How could he discourage her when he couldn't even trust himself? It broke his heart making her feel guilty while he turned his back on her. *But I am Cat's Advisor now. What am I supposed do when she needs help? This is confusing... for both of us.*

He strode down the hallway and silently cursed Brogan for putting him in this predicament.

Eight

After her blunder, Cat had no appetite. She did manage to get dressed, but she mulled over her mistake the entire time. She didn't blame Heron if he wanted to avoid her.

While she clasped a bracelet on her wrist, someone knocked on the door. Heron stood on the other side, no doubt. Catriona held her breath. This would be awkward. She wasn't ready to face him again.

Opening the door, she felt relieved to find Rhys standing there. His presence was a welcome distraction.

"Hello, Catriona. You are lovely today."

"Thank you, Rhys."

"Are you ready?"

"I believe so." She pulled at the hem of her dress. "Do I look OK? I don't normally wear dresses. I'm more of a jeans and T-shirt kind of girl."

He smiled at her. "You are stunning."

Rhys offered his arm, and Cat accepted it gracefully. He escorted her down the corridors. His company was pleasant, although Cat found it difficult to acknowledge him as an Elder. He seemed so young, not someone she envisioned as a god.

As they walked, Catriona thought about the immortals and

their roles. Many things about them challenged her beliefs. Who could imagine a group of gods overseeing the entire universe? But in a way it made sense. How overwhelming it would be for one entity to juggle everything, especially considering the endless possibilities for life on other planets. The multitudes of individuals on Earth, of all races and backgrounds, living together in one tiny world justified the need for an entire network of gods to create and manage the cosmos.

She could sense the immense wisdom and power lying in each of these gods, and yet it didn't seem that one was better than another. Brogan was their leader in name only. All the Elders had strength and wit. Referring to themselves as immortals rather than gods showed no ego. It was humbling.

The dark colors each of them wore puzzled Catriona the most. Didn't the proverbial bad guys wear black and the good guys white? Apparently, mankind's need to come up with a tangible way to distinguish "good" from "evil" didn't extend to the entire cosmos.

"How old are you, Rhys?" she asked, trying to curb her racing mind.

He grinned. "Older than dirt, and dirt is pretty old."

Cat laughed, admiring his sense of humor. She gently squeezed his arm, thinking they'd get along well.

"I am older than your mortal mind can fathom. So for both our sakes, do not even try."

The closer they came to the Cathedral, the more her nerves jumbled like thick knots in her stomach. Anticipation was killing her. Maybe the Council only wanted to ask questions, and she needed to answer them truthfully and be done. And maybe they'd finally explain why she was in the Thirteenth Realm in the first place.

When they arrived, Cat couldn't suppress her surprise upon entering the mystical space. The atmosphere was breathtaking. Tiny multicolored prisms, presumably coming from the sun, danced through the crystal pillars that surrounded the room. The intense live energy vibrated so quickly it made her dizzy. Catriona reached out, catching one in her hand, and marveled at its magnificence.

Catriona felt like a child, elated over a new discovery. She was distracted and spellbound by the multicolored beams, and Rhys had to steady her while they walked down the long marble stairs. She almost missed a step, causing Rhys to catch her, hoisting her back on her feet.

Her face flushed. "Thanks," she mouthed, as her laughter echoed through the room. She spied the other Elders, clothed in their elegant dark attire and exquisite jewelry, sitting in the middle, on the lowest platform in a circle. Each Elder sat like a beautiful effigy, barely moving, as their eyes studied her.

Brogan stood regally in the center of the Cathedral, in the exact spot Heron had stood the day before. The benevolent Council Leader didn't smile, but his eyes were soft and welcoming.

Catriona looked around, not seeing Heron anywhere. She hadn't decided if his absence was a blessing or a curse, but she'd be too embarrassed to look at him anyway.

A tall beautifully engraved golden chair, with cushions covered in crimson velvet, was positioned in the middle of the room. She caught a glimpse of the top of Heron's head peeking out from behind the chair. His seating choice had to be deliberate. Cat inwardly moaned.

Rhys ushered her toward the ornate chair. He motioned for her to sit and squeezed her hand lightly. Then he took his seat next to Maeve, who smiled at Cat and nodded at her dress in approval.

Dresses weren't Cat's first choice, but she felt elegant in the full-length silky plum garment with the scoop neck and cinched waist. Round amethyst jewels adorned her ears along with a matching choker with a few diamond accents, understated but elegant. She had thrown her long brunette hair up into a messy bun; ringlets framed her face. Catriona had never been talented when it came to styling her hair, and this was her half-hearted attempt to look presentable to a group of perfect immortals.

Brogan approached her. "Understand this role is not to be taken lightly. Earth is at a pinnacle point in its evolution and you, as the Observer, by contract, are required to answer and explain any and all questions."

She nodded. "First, will you please clarify why I'm here?"

His lovely voice resonated throughout the sanctuary. "An Observer is a diplomatic position. Although you may not remember this, Catriona, before your birth you agreed to be selected should the need arise." He smiled, stroking his beard. "You were chosen out of hundreds of others. It is now your role to represent Earth by answering questions pertaining to the state of the planet. This portion we are commencing today is called the Questioning, an interviewing process where we consider information pertinent to both sides."

She frowned. "Both sides of what?"

"Both sides of the Thirteenth Realm."

Cat hadn't realized there were two sides. Heron hadn't mentioned it. Had she seen it when they took their walk?

"Are you saying there is another Council of Elders I'll speak with?"

"Yes, although they are not referred to as Elders," Brogan said.

"When do I meet them?"

"Soon," he mumbled.

She sensed his unease. Two sides generally meant opposing forces: opposite beliefs, opposite opinions. This other group probably wasn't nice. Trepidation shot up her spine, and the proverbial walls came up, an instinct she had acquired from having been wrongly accused of many things in her life. It was natural for her mind to be on the defensive, gearing up for battle.

As if someone had detected her inner anxiety, the sedative feeling returned, streaming through her body in intense waves. She wanted to go to sleep.

Yawning, Cat tried to focus, but the little lights began to distract her. One of the small rainbows appeared to be prancing across the back of her hand as if it were alive. Catriona laughed, giving no mind to Brogan, who stood patiently waiting.

She glanced up. "Sorry."

He cleared his throat before continuing. "As your Advisor, Heron will be able to tell us if your answer is true or not."

Catriona peered up at Brogan. *This is serious business.* Heron sat directly behind her, and she could feel his gaze burning a hole through her back. Did he do it on purpose and, if so, why? She'd prefer to at least see him, if for nothing more than moral support.

Her Advisor abruptly appeared at her side, startling her. "I will attest to her statements and verify if they are true."

Cat shifted in her seat. How somber Heron appeared. He didn't even acknowledge her. The giddy feeling faded. The Questioning might be a formal procedure, but this tell-the-truth game appeared less like simple questions and more like an interrogation. All warmth had left the room.

Cat tapped her foot and squirmed in her chair, feeling like something could pop out at her at any moment, and… something did.

Golden ropes sprouted out of the chair, snaked their way around her wrists, and fastened them to the arm rest. She gasped, struggling in an attempt to get free. This was not what she had expected.

"No!" she shouted.

"Do not struggle, Catriona. It will only make them tighter," Brogan warned.

She looked up at Heron's expressionless face. Adrenaline coursed through her. Her mind couldn't fathom what they were doing. She jerked violently every which way, and the golden ropes tightened. She cried out as pain bore down on her limbs.

"Relax, Catriona," Heron said.

She began hyperventilating and glanced over at Maeve, thinking she would be concerned about her welfare, but even Maeve was motionless. The Elders all sat there, stoic.

Being trapped drove her out of her mind. She was like a wild animal, fighting and writhing in frustration, and the ropes only constricted her wrists until they went numb.

"Who the hell are you people?!" she screamed.

No one responded.

"Loosen them!"

Brogan knelt down and looked at her. "I will if you calm down."

Catriona abruptly stopped fighting. Her panting was a testament to her fear. "I want to go home to my family... I don't belong here."

"You *do* belong here, whether you remember it or not." Heron said.

The golden ropes loosened a little but still held her fast. She opened and closed her palms, trying to get the feeling back in her hands. Why were they doing this?

Cat sat with her head against the back of the chair, eyes shut, and wished she were back at the café sipping her latte. *None of this is real. It's a nightmare... breathe.* Focusing hard, she imagined the environment: the smell of coffee, the jazz music. Compared to this, the cold weather and depressing mood seemed like a paradise.

She couldn't ignore her constraints. "Ah!" she cried out. Cat put her head down, sobbing.

"Catriona, you must calm yourself," Heron rubbed her shoulder for comfort. "The rope is necessary. Answer Brogan's questions truthfully and everything will be fine."

"Please get me out of here," she pleaded with tears in her eyes.

"I cannot." Heron looked at Brogan.

The Council Leader stood before her with his hands folded behind his back. "All right, let us begin. First, do you believe in a god?"

"What?" she said.

Brogan leaned forward. "Do you believe in a god?"

"What's that got to do with anything?"

"Everything!" he shouted, inches from her face.

Catriona flinched.

"I'll ask you again, do you believe in a god?"

"Yes," she replied. What kind of sick game were they playing? Did she hear him, an immortal, ask her if she believed in a god?

Brogan continued. "And what kind of a god do you believe in?"

Cat didn't have a clue what they wanted. Hoping Heron would initiate their telepathic communication, she glanced at him, but he refused to look at her. She was on her own.

Cat put her head down. "An all-knowing, wise and kind god." Her voice was strained.

Heron nodded at Brogan. Apparently, he was not only her Advisor, but an official lie detector as well.

"Have you ever cursed your all-knowing, wise, and kind god?" The Council Leader asked.

She hesitated. They had put her in such a vulnerable

position. She said up straight and looked Brogan straight in the eye "You're damn right. Is this my punishment?"

He smiled. "No. We are glad you are challenging your perception of who we are. This is your first test."

If she played it straight by admitting her beliefs in front of all the Elders, knowing what they could do to her, wasn't she being truthful and brave?

The Council Elder's face softened. "Being trapped is one of your fears."

"Understandably." Catriona nodded.

"It is our job to reveal your fears. Bringing your fears out into the open will help you control and eventually overcome them."

Brogan turned his back to her and walked to the platform. "How do you feel about being out of control?"

She looked at the ropes on her wrists. "I hate it."

"Yes, I would say. Last night, when you were not able to leave your chambers, was a test, too. There will be many more. Understand we are trying to help you." He faced Cat. "We are not surprised by your reaction, but before we can get you into a position where you can truthfully answer questions without hesitation, you must get over your fears."

"I don't understand. Why?" she asked.

Brogan strolled toward her, his gentle brown eyes pulling her in. "To prepare you for what is yet to come. You must answer truthfully, regardless of the consequence. There is no protection and no self-preservation for an Observer. Becoming defensive has no place here, which will be difficult for you, Catriona. You are strong willed. Please resist fighting."

She looked at Heron.

"Observers are unemotional, neutral, and composed when answering. Although they express anger, fear, happiness... a full range of feelings, they are not overly emotional about anything,"

Brogan said.

He put his hand on her shoulder. "If you were a true Observer, you would not even flinch at the restraints because you would understand the underlying meaning of it all."

Brogan snapped his fingers and the ropes disappeared. Relief washed over her as she rubbed her wrists.

"You are a warrior with a compassionate heart. Under any other circumstance, this would be applauded, but an Observer must stick to facts... and *not* what you think we want to hear. It is for your own safety. This will test you beyond your breaking point, and believe me when I say the Questioning will tear down barriers you did not even realize you had."

"What do you mean for my own safety?" she asked. "Am I supposed to be afraid of you? Is that what you want?"

The Council Leader smiled. "No, Catriona," his voice was softer. "I do not want you to be afraid of us, but you will be afraid of them."

She frowned.

"This other group calls themselves the Brotherhood. As an Observer you are required to be questioned by both groups, and it is important you understand what to expect. The Brotherhood will not have your interests at heart, not like we do. We are only trying to prepare you, so when you are sitting in front of them, you will be in control."

Cat appeared puzzled. "Control of what?"

Brogan brushed her face with his fingertips. "They will poke at your weaknesses, and your weaknesses are something we cannot allow them to discover. We must desensitize you. Consider the Elders' treatment a form of tough love."

Brogan grabbed her arms and hoisted her to her feet. "Take her to the Stones."

Heron and Rhys were upon her in a blink of an eye.

Gripping her arms, they escorted her out of the Cathedral like a common criminal. Her shoes scraped on the marble floor.

They went down numerous hallways, passing the Oval Room and the one leading to her chambers. They took a sharp right and walked down circular steps. Around and around they went, lower and lower, until they reached the cobblestone floor of the ground level. Torches outlined a dim passageway resembling a tunnel. The moldy, damp air went up her nostrils as they passed several heavy wooden doors with iron latches. This prison looked like a medieval dungeon. They passed numerous doors before reaching the end of the hallway. They opened the last door on the left and heaved her in with such force she slid across the ground, bruising her knees. The door clanged shut behind her.

It was pitch dark. All of her senses went on high alert trying to grasp where she was. More cold, flat stones lay beneath her.

"No, no, no, let me out!" she screamed, but the sound came out of her throat like a whisper.

She got to her feet and lunged in the direction the door had been, but after several steps she found nothing. Twenty steps in this direction, ten steps in another, and still nothing. No matter what direction she went, there were no walls.

A ray of light, through a small gap, struck her face. Through this tiny hole in the wall, she recognized Heron staring back at her.

"Please let me out," she pleaded in a barely audible voice.

He took in a deep breath before speaking. "What are you afraid of? Do you not trust us?"

She ran toward the light. "I did, you sick bastard! Let me out!"

"Catriona, I'm standing right out here." His voice sounded like he was off in the distance. "Answer the question. What are you afraid of?"

She sat down, wrapped her arms around her legs, and

buried her head in them. "I'm afraid... I'm so afraid," she sobbed.

"Afraid of what?" he asked, in a comforting tone.

"Darkness!"

"And why are you afraid of the dark?"

The salt from her tears stung her lips. "I can't see in this void, I can barely hear, I'm in nothingness," Cat wailed. "Please, please... let me out!"

"You hate darkness, do you not? Now you have identified three fears to overcome. Being trapped, out of control, and in the dark. What are you going to do about it?"

"Go to hell!" she seethed, glaring at him.

"I am leaving now."

"No... Don't leave me," she whimpered.

"I will be back, I promise."

The ray of light holding the only hope of getting out of her predicament disappeared, and she was once again in complete obscurity.

Nine

Heron and Rhys returned to the Oval Room to join the rest of the Elders.

Heron sat down and folded his hands on the crystal table. He had no doubt this treatment could go one of two ways for Cat. If she managed to overcome her fears, he'd rejoice. But if not... He tried to force the image of her terrified face out of his mind. Every ounce of Heron's immortal being wanted to comfort her during her distress. This treatment went against his grain and it was the hardest part, thanks to the Elders.

"We are going about this the wrong way." Heron shook his head.

Rhys smiled. "How long will it take to get her over these fears?"

"What she is experiencing could have serious repercussions. It depends."

"It is hard for all of us to see her in this position," Brogan said.

Heron swallowed hard. "Her reaction is like any human's under those circumstances, and all I can do is watch. I am betraying her."

Maeve spoke up. "Breaking her down a little, first, to help her behave like a regular Observer is our mission. It is the only way she stands a chance."

"Let us discuss that now, shall we?" Heron said. "Never mind the fact you all went behind my back changing her Life Chart. Now I am supposed to help you fool the Brotherhood?"

"Why do you suppose we are going about it in this manner?" Brogan asked. "This appears cruel, and it is unfamiliar territory for us all, but you, Heron, are wise enough to see the principal reason. Surely you realize this is the only way?" He stood and approached him. "We are gods who have created humanity from our own DNA, long before the waves of corruption. I want our children, our experiment--"

"An experiment," interrupted Heron, "that went awry eons ago because no one had the courage to intervene. We watch them teeter on the brink of annihilation before calling upon an Observer to tell us the same mind-numbing scenario over and over again!"

"We must let them--."

"Must let them, what?" snapped Heron. "Choose for themselves? Except, how can mankind choose wisely toward a utopian society when they are manipulated by chaotic forces at each turn! They live on a bipolar planet, while we witness everything from a comfortable distance."

Heron shifted in his chair. "Being an Advisor awakened me after witnessing human consequences up close. Let me inform you, it is one thing to witness it and quite different to live it. Time on Earth goes on, societies rise and fall, and it does not matter what the Observers say."

A confused expression splashed across Brogan's face. "You have missed the purpose of all this," Brogan said.

Heron rambled on. "Source agrees, and it all goes back into balance… for a while. Everyone goes about their business until the threshold is breached. Chaos is no longer able to be contained and spins back out of control."

Brogan pondered his words. "It would take centuries to get

humanity back to the stage they are in now. Are you suggesting we destroy them all and start over? The experiment has always been to see where they go, through their own choices."

"But they are not all of like mind, Brogan." Heron shook his finger at him. "There are millions of humans crying for unity and peace. Little progress is made because their voices are lost beneath the shouts of the corrupt, who are currently in power. The Brotherhood is directly responsible!"

"With the technological advancements they have achieved," Brogan said, "it is enlightening to watch mankind's consciousness expand. This phase of the experiment was not shortsighted."

Heron glowered at him. "I understand that, and I want the same thing. But why is it all up to Catriona?"

"Think, Heron," Rhys interjected. "This is a multistep solution. What would be the best way to fix Earth's imbalance on a more permanent basis?"

"She is a surrogate, there to experience the world," Heron said. "That part I understand."

"My friend, you are so blinded by your love for her that you have not thought all of this through." Rhys patted Heron on the back. "If a god directly experiences a human life, they will also know a better way to correct the imbalance. What better way to have a legitimate impact on the planet than to also be an Observer who can correct it?"

Heron's eyes widened. The proverbial curtain suddenly drew back, shedding light on the real reason for Catriona's involvement. "This was your plan from the beginning?"

Brogan glanced over at the empty thirteenth chair, Catriona's chair. He smiled. "Now you understand why our beloved immortal Catriona agreed to do this. She is an Elder, a god, experiencing firsthand what it is to be mortal, and the best candidate to balance the Earth in our favor once she returns. Which is why the Brotherhood must never know."

Heron scratched his head. "I admire your boldness, but do you think letting one of our own be picked will give us any more of an advantage? You are looking so closely at the second step that you are blind to the first. What if she does not pass the Questioning?"

"There is strength within her, and she is good at hiding her feelings," Brogan replied. "Her temperament is in line with an Observer--we need to reinforce it."

Heron shook his head. "I know her better than any of you. As an immortal she is unrivaled, but in mortal form, she is vulnerable. How did you manage to keep the Brotherhood from seeing her immortal abilities while she was on Earth?"

"There were certain points along the timeline when Observers were being monitored. We knew when that would be and made adjustments accordingly," Brogan said.

"Of course it was convenient that I would be too involved watching over her to be aware of these key monitoring points. Why was I not included?"

"Your knowledge of her having been chosen would have clouded your judgment. You would have been a liability," Maeve answered.

Heron arched his brow. "I would never have agreed to it."

"Exactly, and we were aware of that," she replied.

"How did she manage to pass as an Observer in the first place?"

"We depleted her powers when she turned nine years old," Maeve said, "the period when Catriona started remembering who she was. We would never have been able to hide her had we not intervened."

Heron couldn't believe what he was hearing. Their plan had too many flaws. "The human body is genetically engineered by gods. *We* planted our DNA directly into those human cells. Did any of you consider what would happen if an incarnated god connected more to the immortal DNA than to the mortal one?"

Maeve nodded. "Yes, we anticipated it."

"Well, whatever you tried to do never completely diminished her abilities," Heron said.

"That is true, but we suppressed what we could."

"It was not enough. She still possesses a fraction of them. Had you been successful at depleting every one, she would have adjusted better. Now that she is back in the Thirteenth Realm, it is only a matter of time before all her powers return. How do you plan to hide them now?"

The Council Leader rubbed his chin. "We managed to keep her hidden from the Brotherhood this long; now we must continue to do so. It is your job to help conceal her abilities and conceal her true nature for her own protection."

Heron snorted. "She is a powerful god. How am I supposed to suppress her? The longer she stays in this Realm, the greater her chances of remembering."

"Which is why there are measures in place."

"And those would be? We are arguing two sides of the same coin. Maybe she should remember. If Cat is fully aware of her divinity, she can easily fool them."

The Council Leader's stern face proved he did not want to discuss it any further. "Catriona may be in the Thirteenth Realm, but she is still mortal. You cannot choose for her."

"I am not!" replied Heron. "I simply want to give her options. The question remains, is it better for her to stay ignorant of her immortality or not?"

Brogan sighed. "It is better she remains unaware."

"Why?" said Heron, raising an eyebrow. "Did the Brotherhood object when she was chosen as the Observer?"

"No, they agreed," Maeve replied.

"If there had been any suspicion, they would have challenged it the instant she was picked."

Maeve shot Brogan a look.

"What is your end game?" Heron asked.

"After the Questioning is over and she returns to Earth to implement the verdict, we hope she chooses in our favor," Brogan said.

Heron laughed at the irony. "Let me make certain I understand. You want Cat to be ignorant of her immortality, knowing full well in mortal form she will be vulnerable to their manipulation, but somehow she is to overcome all of it and choose a course of action favorable to the Elders because she is one of us?"

"Yes."

He laughed harder.

"Has any Observer ever done exactly as we wished?" said Brogan. "This is our only hope of gaining more influence than ever before."

"Oh, I see. If she passes the Brotherhood's portion, you hope to catch her on the tail end of all this and--"

Brogan banged his fist on the crystal table. "That is quite enough, Heron! Our job is to pass her off as an average Observer, and I say she stays suppressed!"

"This is nonsense! Why are you so adamant about keeping her oblivious?"

Brogan paused, taking in a long, slow breath. "If they find out she is a god during the Questioning, there will be horrible repercussions."

"What do you mean?"

The Council Leader looked at the other Elders around the room. "The outcome may go several ways."

"Explain."

"If the Brotherhood finds out Cat is a god from the Council, they will kill her, forcing her into her immortal state."

Heron scoffed. "I do not see a problem with that. She would be released to return to us. We will write it off as a failed plan with good intentions."

"No, Heron. It may not work like that. They can either forgive her transgression, letting her return as an Elder, and call upon a new Observer... or do something far worse."

"Such as?"

"Once she is in her immortal state, she can no longer hide behind her mortal veil. The Brotherhood may decide to petition Source for retribution."

An ache ripped at Heron's gut. "Source was never aware of all this?"

"That would have meant Source had chosen a side, which it cannot," Brogan said. "We have managed to keep it a secret from Source as well."

Heron's eyes narrowed. "What kind of retribution are they capable of?"

"Source may allow her to fulfill her Observer duties on Earth, but when she returns to the Thirteenth Realm again, she could be forced to serve the Brotherhood as well as the Elders as punishment. That is the Law of Balance."

Heron stood up. "Did Catriona understand the risks before she incarnated?"

The Elders said nothing.

"Did she understand the risks!?"

Brogan sighed. "No, she did not."

The Advisor threw his hands up and clutched his hair in disbelief. Walking around the Oval Room, he peered toward the sky as if begging for an answer.

Rhys stood by his fellow Elder. "I am sorry, Heron. This was precarious on our part, but we needed any advantage for the fate of humanity. It was a risk we were all willing to take."

"Except Catriona!" Heron wailed.

"The needs of the many always outweigh the needs of the few," Rhys replied.

Heron pointed to the thirteenth seat. "The fate of her soul lies on your heads! If that chair sits eternally empty, mark my word I will take matters into my own hands!"

Maeve reached for him, but he pushed her away. "Oh, Heron. Please understand we will do everything we can to make sure that does not happen. She is one of us."

"And yet you are willing to risk so much. You are her closest friend, Maeve. How can you stand by watching this chaos unfold?"

The female god fell speechless.

"I am disgusted by all of you!" When Heron left, the Oval Room shook violently, dissipating furious energy in a million directions.

The Elders glanced at one another.

Brogan turned to them. "I am afraid we have provoked a lion."

Ten

The immortal's wrath knew no bounds. His deafening footsteps echoed throughout the entire Thirteenth Realm. The sky turned gray as thunderous clouds appeared out of nowhere, and people scrambled from the streets to escape the stinging rain and the exploding force of lightning.

Heron shook uncontrollably thinking about all the planning done behind his back. How could the Council allow this plan to be executed without having more control over the outcome?

There was only one place he wanted to be. Wandering down the dimly lit corridor, he made his way toward the Stones. He descended the circular stairway. How could he comfort the terrified woman sitting in the dark? His heart bled for her.

The smell of the Stones made him want to wretch. When he arrived at the door to her cell, a rat scurried across the icy floor. The cold must be brutal for her, sitting, shivering, in the dark. Heron slid down the length of the door onto the cold stones with his hands covering his face. What was he to do?

Every once in a while, a sound from the other side pierced through the silence. He turned his head, and the faint whimpering echo crushed his already heavy heart. He sighed heavily and banged the back of his head against it. The whimpering stopped, then resumed minutes later. He sat, hopeless, in the shadows.

Behind that void sat the immortal mate he had loved for

centuries, although she is not aware of it. They were the perfect embodiment of male and female energy, paired since her promotion into the Council. It was difficult to imagine they'd be in this quandary. He reflected on the day Cat had expressed her desire to incarnate in order to live as a mortal to gain a better understanding of their plight. Heron wasn't too keen on the idea, but he admired her willingness to experience life directly on a third dimensional planet, knowing how difficult it would be living with energies much denser than those in the Realm. He agreed with one stipulation, he would be her Advisor.

Understanding her inability to remember her divinity once she had taken human form, he had watched Cat endure the ups and downs of a mortal life. Heron relished the happier, more joyful times, but during the hardships and trials, all he could do was whisper encouragement in her dreams. Sometimes he would speak to her through the voices of others, offering words of wisdom and comfort.

Being a god, Heron had endless power and could easily manipulate her situation however he pleased, but it went against Universal Law. No infraction would go unpunished, and that rule applied to all gods. Rules were rules, and every immortal had to follow them. Heron wasn't allowed to intervene, but every fiber of his divine being told him he couldn't sit back and do nothing, especially when he could do something.

There must be a loophole. Cat was technically mortal, and the same earthly laws regarding free will applied even if her physical body was in the Thirteenth Realm. It was easier to influence her now that she could hear and see him. Options were available, but choosing for her was not. He thought hard, fighting off the deep anger that had resurfaced. Heron would not lose his goddess.

Any trepidation shown to the Brotherhood would be deadly, especially when they vetted candidates, by using less than ethical tactics, to make sure an Observer was legitimate. What the Elders were putting Catriona through was child's play.

No path Catriona walked down, while desperately searching for answers, was safe. There would be dire consequences either way. Heron remembered what Catriona had asked him when they were at the Blue Crystal Towers.

"What if I give you permission to make a choice for me, can you do that?"

"Only under rare circumstances. So rare, in fact, the choice would have to also directly affect me."

Heron's thoughts were suddenly interrupted by wailing. Cat's pathetic sobs reverberated through the door.

"Catriona," he spoke loudly.

She'd been weeping so hard, she couldn't answer him, only gasp. "Her... Heron?"

Hoping he could comfort her, he put his forehead to the door, speaking in a tranquil tone. "Remember when you were around seven years old, and your friend locked you in a closet as a joke?"

"Yes," she whispered.

"You were screaming and crying, but I could do nothing but sit in there with you, a hidden apparition, trying to console you with my thoughts."

She didn't reply.

"I am forbidden to be in there, Catriona, but I am sending you all of my comfort and love. I need you to visualize receiving it. Can you do that?"

"Yes."

Heron placed his hands on the rustic door, beaming every ounce of solace he could. The energy permeated the wooden barrier, in invisible waves, touching Catriona's heart. She noticed a tingling, warm sensation. She had experienced that feeling on several occasions--it had been Heron who had given it to her.

"Thank you," she whispered again, welcoming his kind intrusion.

"I want you to understand that what you are seeing, hearing, and feeling are tools of human sensory perception, for survival, but you must reach beyond that. You are never alone when you are trapped in the dark regardless of what your senses are telling you. Visualize reaching beyond, and realize I am always here to assist you."

Catriona understood his limitations and was grateful that his welcome presence had touched her within that endless void. To succeed and find her way through, she must deny her senses and not lose focus, or the connection would stop. The ability to visualize and reach beyond normal human perception took her to a whole new level. It was a leap of faith, a knowledge that more elements danced around her, available if she acknowledged their presence and did not depend upon the mortal eye.

It was the same method she had used to see others' futures, a bridge into their space. The energy was the same, but used in a different capacity, an energy beyond basic human capability. She could do this.

"Heron?"

"Yes."

"Why would you go along with what the Elders are doing, knowing I may never trust you again?"

Her words ripped straight through him. "There are decisions being made without my consent. Please do not believe I am enjoying this."

"Tough love, right?"

"Yes."

She sobbed again. "Then what do I need to do for them to

release me?"

Her voice sounded like the little girl he had comforted in days past. "Conquer your fears, Catriona. You are a powerful being, more powerful than you realize. Control your emotions and you will be able to fool everyone."

"What do you mean? I'm only human," she said softly. "How am I supposed to fool immortals?"

Heron sighed. "Oh, my dear Catriona. If you only knew the truth."

A noise came from down the corridor. Heron listened. "My time here must be short. Just answer the questions with as little emotion as possible. Be precise and truthful, but brave. Brogan will be back shortly to check on you."

"OK."

He ran his fingers down the length of the wood and patted it lightly. "I will guide you through all of this, I promise."

His voice trailed off, announcing his departure. She was alone again.

Heron's words had been enlightening, imposing a higher purpose on her current situation. Being trapped in a pit of nothingness scared her beyond all reason, but his words had brought about a revelation. He knew something she didn't, and only her faith and trust in him would get her through.

Catriona also realized her circumstances weren't random. Brogan was going to put her in the Stones either way. For the time being, she needed to be proactive rather than reactive, a position she hated more than anything. With that resolve, she reflected on all of her other fears, knowing she must get a handle on all of them or risk having them exposed and used against her.

As a counselor, Cat knew fear as the mind's inability to fully understand something. The "not knowing" could freeze anyone in their tracks, so Catriona went through a mental checklist. She wasn't afraid of a lot… maybe physical things like spiders, but only to a degree, and who wasn't a bit squeamish about them?

The fears the Elders had spoken of were psychological, and these terrors were deeply hidden. She may not be able to overcome them, but she could learn to control them.

Her reaction depended upon how they exposed her to the stimulus. It could be anything. Identifying every possible one would be tricky, and hiding her fears from immortals, like the Elders, would be impossible. The only place to start was by controlling her mental response and talking herself through it as if she were guiding a child through a gauntlet of terror.

Fear of being trapped and in the dark was easy, but they wouldn't leave her in there indefinitely. Kudos to Brogan for finding the obvious fears. And now that this strategy had been revealed, she could move on to the next one. Pain itself didn't frighten her--it was whatever caused it in the first place. Being put through physical discomfort terrified Cat, but she had a high pain threshold, believing she could mentally dismiss it if she had to. At least until it became unbearable and draining. A horrible notion crossed her mind. They wouldn't resort to torture, would they?

Rejection and severe criticism were things she feared, but they posed no life-threatening consequences. Catriona had dealt with those issues all her life and had reached a certain level of acceptance. She had great mental discipline and used the mind-over-matter technique efficiently.

Betrayal was top on her list. Putting trust in another being, only to have him reject and turn on you, caused more mental damage than anything. That's how she had learned to calculate the moves of others. Perceiving a red flag prior to conflict had become a protective mechanism, an attempt at self-preservation. Nothing was worse than being blindsided. Her gift of observation had served her well through the years. Watching the behavior of others, and understanding their motives, made her such a good counselor.

Sitting in the void, Cat verbalized a checklist and drew upon her strength of perception while she waited for what was yet to come.

Eleven

By the time Brogan, Heron, and Rhys returned to the Stones, Cat was shivering so hard her teeth chattered. She was still afraid, sitting in the void on the cold stones, but Heron's words boomed through her mind, giving her comfort. She would try to be brave.

Brogan opened the small window in the door, allowing a misty beam of light to penetrate the darkened space. Catriona's bright indigo eyes greeted him while the rest of her face stayed shadowed in obscurity.

"Someone has gotten a new sense of determination," he said.

Stinging light poured in from every direction. Catriona threw her hands to her head, attempting to block its brightness. Hands circled her body as Rhys and Heron gently grabbed Cat and pulled her to her feet.

She tried to walk, but she was too shaky from her ordeal. Heron lifted her into his arms and carried her down the cobblestone path and up the circular flight of stairs. When they entered the Cathedral, the Elders were again seated on the marble platform, and the lush red velvet chair sat in the middle. Their sympathetic smiles greeted her.

Heron placed Catriona in the chair, then leaned down to kiss her cheek. For a moment, he stared at her, making her think he was going to initiate a telepathic connection, but he simply looked away and walked behind her to take his seat.

Cat noticed Rhys sitting beside Maeve, clasping her hand in an intimate fashion. His overt affection seemed out of place. Were they a couple? Cat dismissed the thought.

She sat on the soft velvet chair and rubbed her arms before nestling into the cushions for warmth.

Brogan stood in front of her. His awe-inspiring, yet intimidating presence unnerved Cat as she tried to stop her legs from shaking.

Cat studied Brogan, like she had done with her patients. She couldn't help sensing that his behavior wasn't normal. An impression of a kind, gentle being came through and sometimes, when he looked at her, she thought they'd known each other for years.

He was a god, the Council Leader. His strong, intelligent, handsome features seemed incongruous with his role as interrogator. Catriona found it difficult to imagine Brogan, or any of the others, were enjoying themselves during this process. The way his mouth twitched while he waited patiently for her to get comfortable confirmed he was in no hurry. And it was even more bizarre that he gazed at her gently even when his voice rattled her to the core.

"What are you afraid of, Catriona?" he asked, breaking the silence.

Remembering Heron's words, she peered directly into his soft, brown eyes and mentally answered him. *"You know exactly what I'm afraid of, Brogan."*

The immortal appeared deaf to her thoughts. Wouldn't he be able to participate in thought transference too? Cat tried again, focusing harder.

Brogan paused and glanced at Heron, who shook his head.

He turned to the Elders. "It appears the Stones made her mute."

The Elders waited in anticipation. What game were they playing? Nothing made sense. When Brogan turned around, she met his unwavering stare.

"I need you to answer the question, Catriona. What are you afraid of?"

"I'm answering your question," she said in her mind.

"Speak to me!" he commanded.

She stood, pointing at him. "I know you heard me, Brogan."

His brow creased. "Answer the question."

"You're a god, you should know already."

"It is not my answer to give. It is yours, my dear."

"So, I can still make choices? Good, then I choose not to answer."

"That law only works on Earth. You are in my Realm now. Tell me what you are afraid of, or I will put you back in the Stones."

This whole charade seemed a complete waste of her time. Cat wasn't stupid. Why must he treat her in such a degrading manner? This was not Brogan. His behavior wasn't becoming of a Council Leader at all. And Catriona couldn't understand why, for a second, she felt a strong sense of equality to him.

She walked over and leaned in until she was inches from his face. "Then do it!"

Brogan smiled at her and softly stroked her cheek with his thumb. His affection caught her off guard. A spark of respect loomed in his eyes.

"Brave Catriona. Why do you make this hard for yourself? You must contain your anger, and not let it keep you from answering my questions." He snapped his fingers. "Remove her!"

Catriona blinked. "Is this how you treat all your Observers?"

"Please understand this is for your own good," he whispered.

Again, she was snatched and hauled back to the Stones, but by different male Elders. Chamberlin and Dorrell escorted her down, but Heron followed. Catriona sobbed quietly the whole way, knowing she'd endure more torture in the void.

The door to the darkness opened again, but before she was shuffled in, Cat grabbed Heron and held onto him with all her might. "Don't leave me!"

He wrapped his arm around her and spoke softly. "Remember what I said? You cannot get angry, Catriona. You must simply answer the questions and tell him the truth."

"But I thought I needed to be brave."

"Whatever is asked, it cannot upset you. Answer as plainly as you can without any emotion behind it."

Catriona feigned laughter. "I'm not a damn robot!"

Heron stroked her hair. "To be successful, you must go along with it. But instead, you challenged Brogan."

Cat held onto him tighter. "I answered the question with my mind."

"Mortals aren't supposed to communicate telepathically," he whispered in her ear.

"Why not?"

He sighed. "Oh, Catriona, let me explain. All immortals share thought transference by mutual agreement. We can easily turn it off and on. But in order for a mortal to telepathically communicate, the immortal you wish to speak with must first activate you, and only then can you commune with him."

"Like you did to me?"

"Yes, and I was not supposed to do that." He brushed a strand of hair away from her eyes. "Brogan realized what you were trying to do. He does not want to know your thoughts, and he definitely does not want you to know his."

"I tried to initiate with you in the Cathedral."

Heron smiled at her. "Yes, I know. Why do you think I have been sitting behind you?"

"Why are you ignoring me?"

"I have to. Now Brogan is aware of what I have done, and he is not happy with me." He wiped away a tear.

"I'm so sorry, Heron. I'm scared."

He held her. "I must leave you now to ponder your apparent disobedience."

"But you're not leaving me, right? You will be outside that door... tell me you will even if you're not."

"I would never betray you like that, Catriona. I will do all I can to help you, but I must also obey the rules set forth by the Elders."

She didn't want him to let go of her. More tears welled in her eyes. "Why must I go through all of this?"

"I must leave now."

He tried to pull away, but Cat grabbed onto him, forcing Heron to pry her arms loose.

"Please don't go."

His gaze bore into her. "Listen to me. You will get through this, I promise."

He produced a blanket out of thin air and threw it over her shoulders. Pulling it around her head so only her face was visible, he tucked it around her so she could snuggle into its warmth.

"Stay warm," he said. Then the immortal closed the door and disappeared.

As futile as it might be, Cat decided to feel out her prison. She walked several feet, and she still came upon no walls. The room appeared to go on forever into oblivion. She persevered, but still came across no solid object except the cold stone floor beneath her.

She tried to close her eyes to hone in on any tangible object, much like a bat using sonar. She jumped in every direction, yelling, and heard only muted sounds, as if she were inside a bubble. The situation appeared hopeless, and Catriona felt herself getting weaker.

Maybe if she cried out she could persuade Heron to come to her aid. After all, her Advisor was on the other side of that invisible door, somewhere. If she called for him, he must come. Cat yelled for him as loudly as she could, anticipating that the door would open at any moment, but it didn't.

"If you never heard me curse before," she seethed, "listen up, I'm just getting started!"

Like a child stomping away from their parents, Catriona uttered every cuss word known to man. Much of the profanity was aimed at Heron, and when she was done, Cat cursed at Brogan to cover her bases. All the while she kept walking, in any direction--she didn't care. Cat could have been turning in circles for all she knew. It felt good to be mobile instead of sitting on that frigid floor.

Standing outside the door, Heron and the others heard every profane word loud and clear.

Chamberlin covered his ears. "She can be wicked."

Heron began walking away.

"Where are you going?" Chamberlin asked.

"Back to the Oval Room. I am certain Brogan wants a report, and he will want to discuss what she did."

The other immortal cringed. "I do not envy you right now, my friend."

The Elders assembled in the Oval Room. Heron glanced at the thirteenth chair. Brogan wasn't there yet, but it was only a matter of time before he barreled through the door, ready to drill him. He should have known the telepathy stunt wouldn't be a secret for long. Her godly abilities were starting to take form. *How long will I be able to fool her before she figures out what she's capable of?*

The sunlight shining through the stained glass, illuminating spectacular colors, gave the room a cheery radiance in every direction. It was like every other day, except everyone sat deathly silent, no telepathy initiated between them. Heron sat, tapping his finger. *This is the calm before the storm.*

The dynamics shifted the second Brogan appeared. As he strode purposefully to Heron, the energy in the room intensified to an uncomfortable pitch.

"Well, that was interesting! What gave her the idea she could begin thought transference with an immortal?" Brogan looked at Heron. "I *do not* want her trying that little stunt ever again!"

Heron took in a healing breath, looking away. But Brogan wouldn't let him off the hook.

"Now that she is aware of the capability, she will try it with every damn immortal she sees! And *you*, Heron, should know better. You might as well sign her death warrant!"

His comment stung. Heron swallowed hard, but said nothing. It had been a risky move on his part, but Heron had his reasons.

"I thought it might benefit her during her trials with the Brotherhood," he said.

The Council Leader stared at him. "And you trust they will not notice?"

"There are ways to hide it. Catriona needs my guidance, and I am giving it to her."

Brogan leaned toward him. "If you care for your Charge, you must treat her as a mortal! Do not initiate telepathy with her again!"

Heron knew that would be impossible--the benefits outweighed the risks. This wasn't something he would have done impulsively. Heron was, after all, a powerful god himself, who deserved some lenience and respect from the Elders after they had blindsided him. He needed more time to work with Catriona.

"Let us review where we are," Brogan said. "She will be at the Stones for two days, long enough to cause discomfort." He turned to Heron. "I want you to retrieve her and watch her in her chambers."

"No!" Heron gasped, "that will not be--."

"Yes, you will," Brogan interrupted. "After she rests a few days, we will reconvene in the Cathedral. Agreed?"

"Agreed," the Elders chimed in.

"Wait!" Heron yelled. "I thought we decided my time with her would be limited. Why not make Maeve, or any of the other female Elders, attend to her?"

"Her time with the Elders is to be limited. You are her Advisor, and she is your Charge--she trusts you. Keep doing what you are doing. But," he warned, "watch your actions."

Heron stood to challenge Brogan. "You may be our appointed Leader, but you are *not* my superior." His lip twitched in anger. "I am equal to you in every way... remember that."

The Council Leader eyed him a moment before exiting the room.

Twelve

The Stones made it difficult for Catriona to tell morning from night. All she could feel was cold and a gnawing ache in her gut. Occasionally, she'd call out for water, but no one answered. The situation triggered a bout of self-pity. She needed to use the bathroom, but when no one came she had to relieve herself on the floor. This cruel form of sensory deprivation took its toll.

Panic rose in her dry throat. She collapsed on the ground, drifting in and out of sleep, dreaming about her family and the terror they must be going through in her absence. She cried for a short spell, then fell back to sleep only to awake in complete darkness.

Exhaustion resigned her to the void. At one point she thought Heron spoke to her, or was she hallucinating hearing his words of comfort and encouragement? Cat tried to envision him on the other side of the door. Even if he wasn't there, thinking about him calmed her, bringing peace to her tortured soul.

Something stirred beside her on the icy stones, waking her. She floated upwards, numb, but sensed strong arms lifting her and holding her close against a warm chest. Cat smiled, too exhausted to speak. She lay limp in Heron's arms, rolled up in the blanket, allowing herself to be taken away.

Once out of the void, she buried her cold nose in his neck for warmth and to avoid the stinging light. The lulling sounds of his footsteps on the marble floor made her aware she was being taken away to a safer, more comforting place.

Inside Cat's chambers, Heron carefully removed her soiled clothing before laying her into a warm bath. She convulsed from the sudden change in temperature, but after shivering for a few minutes, her body warmed to the water, placating her. Heron's tender hands slid down her body, washing away the grunge that lingered from the Stones.

He poured warm water over her head, and he reached for a slender glass bottle near the side of the bathtub. Heron massaged the lavender-scented shampoo through the silken strands of her hair. Catriona moaned at his gentle touch. He caught a glimpse of the cat tattoo peeking through Catriona's brunette hair. How fitting the symbol was, this emblem of grace, resilience, and strength.

After rinsing away all the soap residue, he swept her into a heavy towel before setting her on the sofa near the fire. Heat from the fireplace kept her warm while he patted her skin dry. Once he was done, Heron dressed her in the same jade nightgown she'd worn before.

"Lie down on the sofa and get warm," he said.

There was a soft knock at the door. Catriona heard Heron exchange words with someone and thank them. It must have been the little man who always brought her food.

Heron busily prepared a plate of assorted fruit. He poured a tall glass of water and offered it to Cat, but she was severely dehydrated and weak. He held the glass to her lips, and water spilled from the sides of her mouth as she drank. He dabbed her moist face.

"Thank you for taking care of me." Her voice cracked into a hoarse whisper.

"You are welcome," he responded.

She watched him. Admittedly, he was the only one who seemed worthy of her, even if she was unsure of his motives.

"What?" he asked.

"I'm not sure about you."

He hesitated before handing over a plate. "I am sure you are not."

After having had no food for a couple of days, Cat sat in silence, eating what she could, but her stomach felt queasy. She handed the plate back to him.

"Done?" Heron asked.

Cat nodded. Her eyelids were heavy, fighting off sleep.

He lifted her gently to him before strolling over to the bed. As if he were caring for a child, he tucked the covers tenderly around her while she dove under the comforter for more warmth.

"Goodnight, Catriona," he said, stroking her tresses.

Within minutes she fell fast asleep.

Heron noticed her breathing was shallow. He knelt beside her on the bed, laying his hands on her head and abdomen. Closing his eyes, he summoned healing energy, and within seconds, his hands began vibrating, becoming hot like coals in a fire.

His touch startled Cat, and her eyelids flew open. "It's nice to be the one healed for a change," she said in a croaky voice.

Heron smiled at the irony. In the Thirteenth Realm, Catriona had been one of their most powerful healers. This had been her forte, and she was a much better healer than he. That's why he couldn't let her enter the Blue Crystal Towers. She had worked there prior to her incarnation, and he was afraid she'd remember.

"What happens to me tomorrow?"

"You are with me for the next several days."

"Good." She yawned.

He smiled at her. "That is good, Catriona, because there is so much I need to teach you before the Questioning resumes again."

She instinctively grabbed his hand. "Keep me out of the Stones," she mumbled.

"Oh, Catriona," Heron whispered. "I will do everything in my power to keep you away from there, I promise."

She grinned, giving in to her exhaustion as Heron's healing touch finally lulled her back to sleep.

He took that opportunity to wrap his arms around her, holding her tight. Embracing Catriona again was soothing, and a moment he didn't want to let slip away. He hid his face in her lavender-scented hair, while a contented sigh escaped his lips. Memories flooded his immortal mind, memories of a life they had shared ages ago.

The next morning, she awoke to find Heron next to her. He'd never left her side, guarding her while she slept.

"Well, hello there, sleepy girl," he said.

His happy demeanor caught Cat off guard. She could only give him a drowsy smile.

He pulled the covers off of her. "Time to get up and eat. It has been a while since you ate last."

"What do you mean? I just ate last night."

Heron frowned at her. "That was almost twenty-four hours ago."

"What?"

"You slept a long time."

The Tiffany lamp was switched on, and moonlight bounced off the sheer curtains. It was evening again.

"Come, there is food for you over here." He offered his hand and escorted her to the sofa, where she found another plate of delectable food.

She snickered. "I can't believe I slept that long."

"You needed it."

She plucked a slice of apple from the plate and chewed on it, noticing the fire was nearly out. Catriona grabbed the metal poker and stoked the ashes, thinking it would be wonderful to see it ablaze.

In an instant, it was.

She lurched backwards. "Did you do that?"

Heron looked confused and reached for the metal poker. "No... I did not."

Thinking nothing more of it, she sat down on the sofa and enjoyed her late night breakfast.

Heron bent down and stabbed at the wood. The flames crackled and popped in the silence.

Cat sensed something amiss. She waited patiently for him to speak, but he seemed miles away.

"What is it?" she blurted out.

Heron turned around. "What do you mean?"

"Oh, come on. I can tell something is wrong."

He laid the poker in the metal stand before taking a seat next to her. "We should be further along than we are."

Cat frowned.

"I have so much to teach you before you return to the Cathedral. As it were, Brogan only gave us three days."

"I'm terribly sorry, but being tortured at the Stones will have that effect on you."

She didn't want to lash out at Heron, not after all his loving attention. "I'm sorry, that was uncalled for."

"I wanted to be outside that door, but I could not respond to you. They were watching."

She crawled into his lap and gave him a hug. "This is so difficult, isn't it?"

Heron sighed. "Yes."

"If I'm going back to be questioned again, what do you suggest I do to pacify Brogan?"

"It is much more complicated than that, I am afraid. There is no simple solution."

"Hmm..."

He broke their embrace. "I am not going to pretend any longer, Catriona. Up to this point, I have followed the protocol the Elders wanted to follow, but there is more you need to know, and we do not have much time."

"Understood."

"Brogan wants me to suppress your thoughts. I want you to remember."

"Remember? Remember what?"

"Remember who you are."

Cat tilted her head. "What do you mean by that?"

"What I mean is..." He seemed to be struggling with his words.

"Yes?"

"What I am trying to say is..." Heron stopped again. He sat stone-faced, without a hint of humor. "Catriona. You are a god."

She used both hands to stifle her laughter. "Now, that's a good one!"

His tone became serious. "All your life, you say you never fit in. You did not relate to others easily. Am I right?"

"Most people think they don't fit in." Catriona was still laughing.

"But you have struggled all your life. A constant reminder

of not fitting in."

"Yes."

"Earth is not your home. You know that."

She stifled another giggle, then shrugged. "I guess so."

"You guess so?" Cat toppled off his lap as he stood. "I have been with you since birth, watching you break down in tears due to your frustration at not being able to understand how humanity ticks. It confuses you. People confuse you."

"You're serious?"

"Yes, I am serious. You pretend to be someone you are not so you can fit in and survive on a planet that is not even your real home."

"What are you saying? I'm immortal... a god like you?"

"Yes, that is exactly what I am saying. And Brogan does not want you to become aware of your divinity for fear the Brotherhood will use it against you, but it would be to your advantage."

"Oh, come on, Heron. Don't tease me. Can't you see I'm fragile enough as it is?"

He reached over to brush her cheek with his hand. "I am not teasing you."

"Stop it!" She swatted his hand away. "Do you think I'm a complete idiot?!"

"Of course not."

She jumped up and walked outside to the terrace. How dare he throw that at her after everything she had endured? Why would he say such things? Was he insinuating she didn't handle things well?

A light breeze blew from over the mountains as the moons once again hovered in the star-filled, crystal clear sky. They appeared close, as if orbiting around each other in an intimate embrace, equal, even though one moon was slightly higher in the sky than the other. Lit torches on the terrace cast shadows around her, and the scent of flowers infused the space. It could have been a blissful moment had she not been so aggravated.

Cat stood shaking, taking in deep breaths; she was close to the breaking point. They were all crazy! How much more could she take?

She watched Heron's shadow skew against the marble wall, marking his intrusion, and spun around. "Leave me alone!"

Dismissing him with a grunt, she turned back to face the mountain, letting the cool air wash over her. Meditating on more calming thoughts, she tried focusing on her breathing, but chatter sprung into her mind. Heron stood behind her, in silence, biding his time.

"I said leave me alone!"

Heron approached, grabbed her waist, and held it gently. His mouth was poised inches from hers. "You cannot tell me you are that ignorant. You have insights about others they themselves do not even realize. These gifts of sight and healing are abilities not bestowed upon the average human."

She turned her head. "Many people have similar gifts. That doesn't make me a god."

He stepped back, grabbed her face, and stared deeply into her eyes. "Why are you being so defensive? Listen to my words, Catriona. You are a god, like me. You decided to incarnate to help humanity during this phase of Earth's imbalance--."

"I don't want to hear this!" She twisted away and tried to retreat.

"You must listen to me." He held her fast.

Cat shot him a look of defiance, and he slowly released her.

Catriona ran back inside and bolted for the door, but it was locked... again.

"Stop doing that!" she screamed.

When he caught up to Cat, he tenderly picked her up and

flung her over his shoulder.

"Ah! I'm so pissed at you!" She wailed and kicked. "I don't want to hear any more of this shit!"

He dumped her back on the sofa and stared at her. "You will hear me out!"

She folded her arms across her chest and stared at him.

Pacing back and forth, Heron ran his hands through his dark hair. He knelt beside her. "The Council allowed you to incarnate, to live like a mortal, so you could better serve and understand humanity."

"No," she said softly, shaking her head.

"Yes. You are a lighthouse in a storm, using divine power to guide lost souls safely to harbor. It is who you are, a god. And you chose it."

Her eyelids were closed. Tears trickled down her cheeks.

Heron turned toward the fireplace. "The poker did not stoke that fire; you did with your thoughts."

Cat said nothing.

Heron sat next to her and encircled her in his embrace.

"If I'm a god like you..." Her voice was muffled against his shoulder. "Why haven't I regained all my powers?"

He kissed the top of her head. "There are a couple of reasons. As a mortal, you are bound to that existence until physical death. You are, in every sense of the word, human."

"What are the other reasons?"

"The Council is suppressing your memory, and they have been doing so since you were a child. Understand it is only because they are trying to protect you. They are your friends, and equals."

Cat sat up, wiping her eyes. "You mean to tell me I'm an Elder?"

"I did say 'god.'"

"Why would they treat me like this, sending me to the Stones?"

"What the Elders are doing is *nothing* compared to what the Brotherhood will do. They are trying to prepare you for the worst. But I believe it is important for you to remember your immortal abilities, so that you can protect yourself and be successful during the Questioning. That is why I am at odds with Brogan."

Cat sighed. "I don't want to meet this Brotherhood. They sound horrible."

"Yes, but they are gods as well, equal in every way. And the Council and the Brotherhood have always been at odds."

"Why?"

Heron shrugged. "We disagree about the state of the Universe, and everything housed within."

"Gods disagreeing... huh, I thought that was only in Greek mythology. It makes me wonder who the hell is in charge here."

"Source is in charge."

Cat scowled.

Heron leaned over and planted a kiss on her cheek. "Take a deep breath, and I will explain everything."

Thirteen

She sat on the plush sofa, staring into the fire, as she contemplated everything Heron had said.

Truth was in his words, but part of her still wasn't sure if it was all an elaborate story to set her up for something else. Right now, her psyche was too delicate for any more games.

Heron poured a glass of red wine. "Here, you will need this."

"Wait... there's more?" Cat gulped the wine down in preparation for whatever came next, thinking it best she not be completely sober. Desperate to believe, with all her heart, that Heron wasn't fooling her, she had always held back a little.

Her Advisor refilled the glass.

His story was ridiculous. Did he honestly expect her to trust everything he had said? She listened, amused, if for no other reason than to see what else the Elders might have put him up to.

Heron knew her faith in him had crumbled. To Cat it was all fantasy. Maybe he needed to switch up tactics. A story on a more personal, relatable note was in order.

He stood with his back to her. "What went through your mind when you woke up and noticed leaves stuck to the bottom of your feet?"

Cat's eyes widened. "Something happened. I don't know exactly what."

Heron turned around, grinning at her.

"Are you taunting me?" she asked.

Heron looked away, but the smile never faded from his lips.

"Well, as my Advisor, and from the grin on your face, I assume you have all the answers."

He gestured toward her. "No… please, tell me."

"Fine. It happened when I was young, about five years old--."

"No," he interrupted, "you were nine."

"Are you sure?" Cat asked.

"Yes, I am."

She continued. "I remember it had rained so hard, you could hear the water hitting the roof and coming down the drainage pipes."

"There was no rain." He stifled a laugh. She was testing him, trying to throw him off. Cat had no idea he heard all her thoughts... god help him when she did.

"You're right. It was snowing."

"Nope, no snow. It was mid-October."

Cat smiled. "A huge orange harvest moon hung in the sky outside my bedroom window, so bright the reflection bounced off the trees and grass."

"Correct," Heron said.

"I was supposed to be in bed, but I couldn't resist going into the backyard to dance. I was twirling around and laughing, completely naked."

"Wrong, you wore the long white nightgown with the baby blue bow your grandmother bought you the Christmas before."

She paused. "Yes, Heron."

"Continue."

"The air was so refreshing that October night, I just wanted to dance and dance. I felt peaceful, and connected to everything. Does that make sense?"

He nodded.

"I was happy, but a little anxious, as if waiting to see someone I hadn't seen in a long time."

She stood and meandered toward the fireplace. "But it got late, and no one came. I went back to bed before my parents caught me. When I awoke the next morning, there were leaves stuck to my feet." Cat smoothed her hair. "And the strange thing is, I don't remember going back outside."

"How were you the next morning?"

"My mind was fuzzy. My mother asked if I was all right. I remember sitting at our kitchen table, staring at the wall in a daze. When I finally snapped out of it, it was after noontime."

"Did you notice anything else?"

"I felt disconnected, and sad."

"Why were you sad?"

"Everything seemed different after that." She whispered, "I lost something... a piece of me."

He stood behind her and caressed her back, "Do you want me to tell you what happened?"

"Yes, the memory haunts me."

"I will tell you, but understand I only recently found out the details myself. There is much more that led up to that evening."

Heron seemed to be choosing his words carefully. "You were born with a "caul," or the Seventh Veil. It is a thin piece of membrane covering a baby's face when it is born. It is not common, and to the Universe it signifies divine energy and a telltale sign of special talents."

"I've heard that before, but I figured it was an old wives' tale."

"That is because no one truly understands the significance of it."

"Oh." Cat settled back on the sofa.

"As you got older, you saw how different you were from the other kids. You were not weird, but your thought processes and perception of the world were not similar. It became disturbing, and once your immortal abilities surfaced, it only added to the confusion."

Cat shifted toward him. "My abilities cannot possibly be of the same caliber as a god's."

"Oh, but they are. In mortal form you possess the same gifts, but to a lesser degree. That is why the Elders appeared to you later that night to try to erase your powers."

"Why would you agree to let them?"

"I did not. I understood their visits to be purely benign, simply to check up on you at certain intervals in your life. I had no knowledge of what they were doing. But your talents were never completely suppressed."

She stared into the crackling fire.

"You intuitively knew they were coming, that is why you felt such expectation... It was a celebration in your mind, as if awaiting a visit from long-lost relatives."

"But they never came, Heron. I would've remembered."

"They did come... long after you were asleep. You were in a type of trance, to avoid frightening you while you stood outside under the huge oak tree. An energy shield pulled you safely through the branches as you ascended, concealing everything in case someone happened to be watching."

"Like an alien abduction, in a spaceship?"

"Somewhat. They used a holding craft."

Catriona shivered. "Why didn't they beam me here?"

"Children's minds are too fragile to zap them physically into another dimension. The Elders came to you. When they were finished, you were returned safely to your bed."

"So, the leaves came from the oak tree?"

He intertwined his hand in hers. "Yes."

"Why did they want to erase my abilities?"

"At certain integral times in your life, the Brotherhood monitored you. Since the Council wanted you to be picked, they had to intervene."

"I was being watched all this time?"

"Your godly gifts were blooming. The Elders felt, in order to protect you, they must erase them, forcing you to adapt to the lower energies of the planet, keeping you grounded and hidden."

"And you're saying I agreed to all of this?"

Heron nodded.

"But if I wanted to incarnate as a human, of what interest is it to the Brotherhood?"

Heron's sapphire eyes gazed intensely into hers. "Your story is twofold. Not only did you want to experience a mortal life, you also agreed to be an Observer. Although there are many Observers at any given time, you were the one chosen."

Cat shook her head. "I don't even understand what an Observer is. Why me?"

"Only the immortal Catriona can answer that."

"Doesn't an Advisor help plan their Charge's life? If it's so dangerous, why did you agree to go along with it?"

"I did not. There were two Life Charts floating around."

A scowl creased her forehead. "What's a Life Chart?"

"I'll explain later. Look out onto the terrace. Do you see the torch there to the right? I want you to snuff it out."

Catriona stared at him. "How am I supposed to do that?"

"With your mind."

Cat peered through the sheer curtains that hung over the doorway and focused her thoughts on the torch to the right. She visualized the flame going out, and she concentrated hard. Within a split second, it was out.

She gasped. "No way!"

"You have the ability, Catriona, but can only harness a fraction of your divine energy into flesh. The human body is not a complimentary vessel. Imagine what power you hold as a god."

The thought intrigued her. Looking around the room, she sized up other objects. Her attention went to the flames burning in the fireplace. Again, by focusing her thoughts, she extinguished them.

"Wow!" She laughed, looking at the Tiffany lamp.

"No, no. Don't get too overzealous."

Her mouth twitched. "How are my immortal gifts coming back?

"I did something." He smiled.

"What did you do?"

"I performed a ritual in the Cathedral. Your immortal energy is now acclimating to the Thirteenth Realm, to a lesser degree, of course, but enough that you are able to exercise your powers with intent."

Catriona tried to come to terms with this idea. "Do the Elders know my powers are coming back?"

"No, that is why we must be even more careful."

"If I volunteered to be an Observer, then surely I can handle myself."

"You have no idea."

"After what I went through in the Stones, I'm quite capable." She rolled her eyes.

Heron grabbed her chin. "Dear soul, you do not understand. You are in over your head."

"Then why did you tell me all of this?"

"I will show you."

Heron's gaze locked onto hers with such force she couldn't look away if she wanted to. The dizzying sensation intensified, a burst of white light zoomed, and she saw a panoramic view of laser-sharp images in her mind. The scene was from an odd point of view, but soon she realized they were Heron's memories.

In the first image, Catriona sat at the crystal table in the Oval Room speaking with the other Elders. Wearing a silky dark dress, in the same style as the rest of the female Elders, she looked similar to her mortal self, yet different. Instead of her full brunette locks, her tresses were golden blonde and pulled back in a braid with thin silver cord. A few strands hung down, framing her face. A huge silver necklace, shaped like a half-moon, hung midway down her breasts, and shiny silver bracelets twisted around her arm, going up to her shoulders.

Catriona gasped at her graceful, unblemished appearance.

Although The Council were communicating telepathically, a heated discussion had some of the Elders shaking their heads. The desperate tone of the conversation resonated in the divine ones' minds.

The immortal Cat's calm demeanor shifted to anger. There was a sense of urgency, something unforeseen. A decision had to be made about which the Elders clearly disagreed. The mood wasn't a happy one, and Catriona realized those feelings came from Heron.

Suddenly, the scene disappeared. Cat blinked at him, wondering why the image had left so quickly, but Heron shook his head, as if to say he didn't want to linger on that particular vision too long.

The next scenario was a room filled with shimmering golden light. Its blinding brightness was akin to looking directly at the sun. This place seemed familiar, and Cat recognized the room as part of the Blue Crystal Towers, even though she had never been inside.

She saw herself dressed in a fitted violet floor-length gown. The straps tied behind her neck, and the V-neck fabric hung above her breasts. This immortal version of herself seemed much more competent than the Cat she knew.

She stood over a person lying on what appeared to be an operating room table which hovered in the air. This troubled soul had crossed over to the Thirteenth Realm, and it was Catriona's job to administer healing energy by laying her hands on him. The individual needed to be cocooned in pure light to heal from trauma.

Heron's memory skipped again.

Catriona moaned, wishing she could observe longer.

The last vision showed Heron and Catriona sitting together in the Cathedral. They appeared to be discussing the parchment scroll she held in her hands. Seeing herself through Heron's eyes revealed his true admiration for her. They had a close bond, an attachment that wasn't just an Advisor/Charge relationship.

The pair appeared to be going over plans for her incarnation, but an argument broke out. Heron pointed out the ramifications of some of the things written on the parchment, but Catriona pleaded her case. Her intentions of going through with the task were clear. Heron had apprehensions. Catriona appeared to be begging for his approval. Something about this image wasn't quite right.

What stake did he have? They were both Elders and creator gods. Maybe they had argued over logistics, or maybe it was normal for an Advisor and Charge to disagree during the planning process. Cat wasn't certain. Regardless, the desperate tone of this scene gave Cat the impression the relationship ran deeper.

"I am going," said immortal Catriona.

"It will not be as enjoyable as you hope," Heron warned.

She touched his shoulder. "I realize that, but it is mine to experience. A mortal life is a tiny flash in the cosmos, I will only be gone a short while. You will still be with me."

"I fear for you," he said.

Catriona smiled. "I know, my love, but I will be back with greater knowledge and understanding."

He leaned over and kissed her with such passion it made the mortal Catriona blush. This revelation proved their relationship was much more than her Advisor had originally let on.

Heron immediately broke visual contact, and the scene vanished. He stood and walked away from her.

"Wait, don't leave," Cat said.

Her Advisor stood at the door refusing to face her.

"Please, Heron. Come sit down."

He turned around. "I am sorry you saw that. It is not..." his face twisted. "All I can say is, an explanation will be offered at a later time."

"All right," she muttered. She wasn't going to push the issue.

"The truth you need to consider right now is you are one of us."

She nodded, forcing a smile. "An immortal... and yet I don't remember any of it?"

Heron sat back down. "A human mind only uses a small percent of its total capacity. Your essence, your energy, is confined. There is no way for you to acquire full abilities until you are separated from your mortal body."

"But we don't die."

"No, we do not."

"What was the benefit of leaving the Thirteenth Realm to live a meager human existence?"

"It is your compassion for creation. You felt compelled to assist humanity on a more individual basis."

She looked into his eyes. "Oh, Heron. What am I supposed to do?"

"We will figure it out." He put his arm around her.

"Thank you."

He kissed her forehead. "You are welcome."

She wanted to stay with him longer, but he stood.

"Tomorrow I will return, and we will start working on how to conquer this Observer role. Until then, I leave you with your meal and a good night's sleep."

"But I've been asleep almost a whole day. Don't you want to get started now?"

He turned around. "The first step for you, Catriona, is to remember and identify with who you are. I gave you a glimpse, but the rest is up to you. I would highly recommend paying attention to your dreams tonight. I am sure they will be enlightening."

"I don't think I can go back to sleep."

"You are already starting to recall things. It will come more easily, but please heed my advice. Do not let anyone know what I revealed to you. Brogan and the Elders believe it is safer thinking you are merely mortal."

Cat nodded. "OK."

Heron opened the large wooden door. "One more thing. I know how your mind ticks. Promise me you will not practice anything by yourself. I should be with you to help monitor it."

"Agreed."

He pointed at her. "I am warning you."

"OK. I understand."

He turned to leave.

"Heron?"

He faced her again.

"We'll also need to discuss what happened between us in your last vision."

He gracefully bowed and left the room.

Fourteen

The next day brought about a bit more clarity. Catriona recalled more of her godly nature. Her dreams were lucid, evoking visions of various places she'd seen before, some from the Thirteenth Realm, including images of the Blue Crystal Towers.

The Towers, as they were called, were among the most elegant buildings in the Realm and commanded respect from all, not for the healing energy they projected into the atmosphere, or the beauty of the crystal structure itself, but for the miracles performed within it.

Anyone who worked there wore the color violet, to signify they were the designated healers. Well-regarded and addressed with the utmost admiration for their exclusive abilities, their talents weren't just administered to mortals who had crossed over. They could heal any biological thing: animals, plants, water, even the air. They could manipulate and change almost anything they wanted, including transforming negative energy into a form conducive to life and growth. It all had to do with the pitch, vibration, and frequency of the force which allowed them to do all types of transformations.

Although all creator gods have the ability, to varying degrees, only a handful are adept at completely restoring--or destroying--*all* things, depending upon their intent. Gods with this specialized skill were revered for their expertise. Catriona was part of this faction, and an extremely powerful immortal.

While she dreamt, Cat saw herself performing intense healings on humans which, upon her awakening, evoked a deep desire to return to the Towers that were beckoning her. She considered sneaking out, but it would be impossible.

A restlessness plagued her, and she paced around her chamber. She needed to experiment, against Heron's wishes. At first it was something familiar, like lighting and extinguishing the torches, but that quickly became boring. She graduated to moving objects around with pure thought. Giggling, she shifted a perfume bottle from one side of the bathroom vanity to the other. It slid back and forth until it accidentally flew off onto the marble floor, bursting into a million pieces. The skill was amazing, and it took little effort.

Subduing her divine potential proved difficult, especially because these feats required nothing more than self-will and intent. As if discovering her telepathic abilities weren't exciting enough, now her body responded to her surroundings by vibrating like a tuning fork. There was a lightness to her form, a transparency of sorts, a feeling of being completely different.

With much enthusiasm, she stood in the middle of her chambers wondering what else she could do. Cat visualized herself levitating off the ground and fixed her attention to the task. At first, she only hovered a few inches, but she focused harder until she levitated five feet off the ground. Pushing her limits, Cat rose higher into the air until she touched the ceiling with her fingertips. Wondering if her talents allowed for more mobility, she zoomed over the top of the canopy bed. Learning to move sideways instead of up and down was too much fun, and it entertained her for hours.

She approached each experiment with caution, not only for her sake, but for Heron's as well. She respected the fact that he had risked going against the Council to explain her authentic nature, and for that, she absolutely adored him. But why couldn't she practice in a safe environment if she had the ability to do it? It was like putting a piece of juicy bubblegum in a child's mouth and telling her not to chew.

Being alone for such a long period of time had proved beneficial, but she missed Heron's company. By exposing the truth, he had fostered greater trust and appreciation between them. Suspended above her canopy, daydreaming of Heron, warmed her heart. At one point, she talked herself into revealing her newfound talents, but her inner voice answered with a resounding, *hell no!*

Catriona shifted her attention to her purpose as an Observer. From what she had gathered, an Observer sounded like an emotionally stunted individual, with almost robotic mannerisms. How could she act that way? Cat wasn't an emotional woman. She had an even temperament, but there were occasions when circumstances irked her to the point she couldn't contain herself. Sometimes her face flushed blood red with anger, or tears of extreme frustration or sadness poured down her cheeks. She was human, and the Elders had witnessed that part of her.

If wearing a poker face was required for this task, it would take time to master. Why would she agree to be chosen as an Observer in the first place? The whole ideal of saving the world seemed a position of martyrdom. She wasn't Joan of Arc and had no desire to be. Her mantra for dealing with everything in the cosmos was "live and let live." It was a survival technique, but it was a mantra nonetheless.

Cat's immortal wisdom must be strong enough for her to succeed. Her faith she would make the right choice for herself, even if the outcome was unforeseen, must prove she was a clever god. She had to control her own fate. And gods don't fail... do they? Otherwise, why go through all of this? With Heron's help, she'd be able to fool the Elders... and the Brotherhood.

Catriona was floating high above the canopy, so deep in

thought she didn't hear the voice vibrating through the wooden door.

"Catriona, are you awake?"

Heron's intrusion broke her concentration, sending her spiraling downward through the thick canopy frame and sheer fabric until she landed on the bed.

"Ouch!" A piece of wood had scraped her thigh.

Heron heard the commotion and knocked frantically on the door. "What is the matter? Are you all right?"

"I'm fine. Just a second."

She rubbed her leg, then walked gingerly to the door and began opening it, but Heron shoved it open and walked past her. He looked worried. He spied the broken canopy lying in a heap on the bed.

His brow arched. "Is everything all right?"

"A hum," she said, hiding her pain.

"What were you doing in here?"

"Nothing, I had a restless evening," mumbled Cat, wiping the sweat from her forehead.

He looked at the canopy and back at Cat. "Hmm... I see."

Catriona walked over to the cart and poured herself a glass of water. She was parched from all her supernatural dabbling.

Heron flashed his bright smile. "You are a vision to behold."

"Oh, thank you," she said between gulps. "I thought this would be appropriate."

Catriona wore a navy wraparound cotton dress that fell below the knee. Small silver hoop earrings and a silver chain accompanied it. It felt comfortable and practical. A testament to her mood as of late.

An awkward silence fell between them.

When she thought about it, Cat found it odd the clothing in her closet kept disappearing. Most of the elaborate dresses she had rummaged through upon her arrival were now gone, as well as the fancy jewels. Had Brogan done something to spite her? Catriona mentally waved it off. All the finery had probably been a ploy anyway. She preferred jeans, camisoles, cotton shirts, and blouses. She wasn't high maintenance.

"Well." He motioned toward the sofa. "Come, sit."

With drink in hand, she followed her Advisor, noticing how well put together he appeared this morning. Rather than his standard gray button-down dress shirt and black pants, he wore a crisp white shirt with a casual beige jacket and pants. The neutral colors accented his medium skin tone and dark hair. The immortal looked astonishingly handsome. A proud smile curved her lips.

He was looking Cat up and down too, but he said nothing. She wondered what he was thinking. Then he abruptly turned his head and coughed before facing her again. He had a mischievous look on his face.

"What?"

Scooting closer to her, he put his finger to her lips. "Do not say anything."

Cat nodded.

He met her gaze, and their mental connection snapped together instantly.

"This seems to be getting easier."

Heron smiled at her. *"Yes, it is, but I have a confession to make."*

"What is it?"

Heron paused. *"From the first time I initiated our telepathy, I have been able to read your mind."*

She rolled her eyes. *"Wonderful. Is nothing private anymore?"*

"I am sorry, please do not be angry with me."

"What if I don't want you in my head all the time?"

"If you wish me to stop, I will. The time has come to get everything out in the open before we continue any further."

"Well, that's thoughtful. I'll send an invitation when I want you digging through my personal thoughts."

Heron grinned. *"Desire noted, and I will honor it. From this point on, we need not formally initiate it anymore. It will be our permanent link of communication. When you want me to be privy to your thoughts, call my name out in your mind."*

"I understand."

"Good," he said aloud.

"How do you switch back and forth so easily?"

"Practice. We will speak as much as possible and only use thought transference when we need to. I promise you will get used to it." He shifted in his seat. "Now onto more important things. The Observer. Who they are, and what they do, is the first part of this lesson."

She positioned herself comfortably.

"An Observer is an incarnated soul from a delegate race in another dimension of beings. They hold no vested interest in the outcome of a planet. Regarding Earth's history, Observers were first introduced back in the 1940's when it was feared without intervention, mankind would annihilate itself."

"I can believe it."

"When the imbalance is too strong to be ignored, an Observer is selected to discuss earthly matters with the Elders and the Brotherhood, prior to an agreement being reached. A course of action is voted upon and implemented, and all goes back to normal."

"Nothing on Earth is normal." Cat took a drink.

"I understand why you believe that, but there is as much abundant good as there is evil."

She sighed. "There are too many people causing too many problems. Humanity seems distracted from the real issues."

Heron agreed. "As gods, we can influence humanity in many different ways, but the ultimate decision is up to Man."

"It sounds like a contest to see who can influence humans the most."

"No, Catriona. We do not view human life that way. Earth is naturally a planet of opposites. Up, down; left, right; good, evil; the list goes on. Persuasion from both groups of gods is required to varying degrees. That is how Source desired it."

"Why would this 'Source' want that?"

"It is about experiencing."

She frowned. "How ridiculous. No one wants to suffer."

"Souls wish to experience many things."

"Unless you're the one suffering the negative consequences."

"Do those consequences help you grow and learn?" Heron asked.

"Sometimes, but not always. A person can be caught up in a pattern of bad choices."

"Exactly. Everyone has a choice. No one can escape choosing."

Cat took another sip of water. "Give me an example of these varying degrees of good and evil, please?"

He put his hands on his knees. "Let us say there is a can of white paint and a can of black paint. Both are pigments with separate qualities, each is unique, but when you mix them, they make many shades of gray. You can no longer see the white or the black, they are combined into another color altogether. Humans are a mixture of both. There is good and evil in everyone. It depends which they choose to be, and to what degree."

"Who is Source?"

"It is a pure, living static energy responsible for creating the Universe. This all-knowing Source is one huge conscious entity all life stems from. Creator gods are sparks thrown off from Source, made to invent and design all forms of life. Once a creator god finishes all we care to create or contribute, we can go back to this static energy we came from."

She smiled. "So, even gods have an expiration date?"

"Technically, yes." Heron laughed. "We do not 'expire' or cease to exist, we return to whole consciousness. It is like going from ten percent of your brain to one hundred percent. Energy never dies… it just changes. You are who you are, only more."

"I still don't understand what it is."

"Source created the Universe, but creator gods create life within the Universe. We are granted the ability to design and manifest for Source."

"Does this ability apply to the Brotherhood?"

"Absolutely."

Catriona shook her head. "Source is being too lenient."

"That is not for me to say."

She smiled.

"Mortals can also manifest things in their lives. Of course it is not of the same caliber as what a god wills into existence, but your thoughts create experiences. What you think, you become." He turned toward her closet and pointed. "You noticed many of the dresses you originally found in there are now gone."

"I thought Brogan took them to spite me."

"No, you did. Being in the Thirteenth Realm allows you to manifest the best possible environment for yourself. Clothing reflects your personality, and you are most comfortable in practical, easy wearing clothes. Expect to see more changes in the coming days."

She laughed. "Well then, expect to see me in nothing but

jeans and T-shirts real soon."

"I do not mean only clothes." His endearing smile caught her off guard. "You will be manifesting your environment based on your beliefs. This will directly affect the Questioning process as well."

"Are you telling me I can control my situation during this whole ordeal?"

"That is exactly what I am saying. When you are afraid, you will draw more fear toward you. When you are calm and focused, you will draw more of that toward you. Like equals like."

The concept finally dawned on her. "Oh, OK."

"The whole reason for putting you in the Stones was to evoke your fear and anger. Which you displayed well."

"Thanks… I think."

What epiphanies did you discover?" he asked.

She snickered. "How pissed off I can get."

Heron gently ran his fingers through Cat's hair, which now appeared much lighter than it had the day before. "We had to break you down a little. That is why the Elders put you there, to prepare you for the worst. Brogan is not the monster he appears to be."

"I sense that about him," she replied.

"The Brotherhood, however, will use every trick to test you. If you show fear or anger, they will surely discover you are not an authentic Observer, and I do not know what they would do to you if they found out."

Cat heard the hesitancy in his voice, but she trusted his judgment. He was still holding something back, but she had to have faith all would be revealed at the right time.

She looked up and held his gaze. "Then we mustn't let them."

Fifteen

Exactly three days had passed since Catriona had sat shivering in the Stones. The thought of resuming the Questioning put knots in her stomach, but she'd been working on controlling her emotions.

Practicing her superhuman abilities allowed her skills to come back almost immediately, and they were becoming stronger and more precise. She had been asleep, and now awakened, expanding far beyond anything she could imagine.

She sat at the dressing table, in the walk-in closet, staring at herself in the jewel encrusted mirror. Something was different. Her skin had a peachy glow unlike anything she'd seen before. She touched her face; the skin appeared toned and supple, with not one wrinkle anywhere. The lovely red ripeness had returned to her pale lips, and her soft, shiny hair was lighter, almost a golden honey-blonde. Even her eyes seemed different, taking on a lighter shade of blue. Overall, she appeared years younger.

While admiring herself, she sensed a presence at the chamber door. No one had knocked, but Cat knew someone was there. She approached the door, standing inches away, and paused. An intense, yet apprehensive energy vibrated through the wooden portal. Cat snickered under her breath. Heron thought he was sneaky. Each of them stood, waiting on the other.

A voice abruptly boomed in her mind.

"I know you are there--are you going to let me in?"

"Maybe," she teased.

"It would be thoughtful if you would reconsider."

"Why don't you huff and puff, and blow the door down?"

"I can get into your room anytime I want. The door is only a formality."

She laughed.

"I am checking to see how well you perceive me out of the room."

"Pretty well, but I sensed your presence long before you said anything."

"Wonderful, may I come in?"

She swung the door wide and smiled at him.

He brushed past her and turned around to offer her his arm. "We need to speak aloud as much as possible. Someone may be watching. Do you care to join me on the terrace?"

She cheerfully went with him.

Standing in the brilliant sunshine always filled Cat with awe of its glory. The limitless sky captivated her, and although the sun always seemed to be shining here, the temperature was never too hot or cold. It sometimes rained, but it was never an all-day event. Even the plants and flowers in paradise needed a good soaking every now and again.

Heron gazed at Cat. "It seems the Thirteenth Realm agrees with you. You are looking godlier every day."

"Thank you."

Cat was a vision dressed in a mid-length silk ruby dress with silver teardrop earrings; she had skipped the necklace. The sunlight fell on her long wavy hair, and her shiny tresses glimmered with three-dimensional color. Hues of brown and gold gently swayed with the caressing wind. Her skin appeared touched by the sun, and her eyes, now light blue, glittered like the ocean. The pale, tired Catriona had blossomed into magnificence.

Heron's fingers touched her cheek. "Oh, I am sorry. I could not help myself. You are a most stunning and radiant creature."

"I guess it's been some time since I appeared this way."

"Yes, some time."

Cat's lips curved into a smile. She enjoyed his touch and secretly wished they could do more. "I'm enjoying this new vitality. I don't feel achy and worn out like I usually do."

"That is good to hear, but I have always considered you beautiful, even in your mortal state." He grinned at her. "All right. We need to focus on the task at hand. Do you have any questions before we resume the Questioning?"

"I have one question."

"Yes?"

"What will the Elders say when they see my transformation? Won't they know that I know what's going on? I don't look the same as I did when I first got here."

"Correct, you do not. Brogan anticipated this. Allow him to give you some other logical explanation should the topic come up."

"What about the Brotherhood?"

"They have not seen you yet."

"But they saw me before... on Earth."

"Yes, but everyone who enters this Realm physically changes a little, although your transformation is much more dramatic than most. They only saw you from a distance when you first arrived. That is one reason why you stayed in the Elder Temple."

"Oh." She seemed to be focusing on her breathing.

"Good, breathe. It will be useful during your responses.

Pause and breathe if you need to buy time."

"There is no time here."

Heron grinned. "You know what I mean. Come, I will escort you to the Cathedral."

A gust of wind blew past, causing a strand of hair to fall into her eyes. Heron gently swept it aside and tucked it behind her ear. His warm hand lingered on her neck. "Are you ready?"

Cat welcomed his comforting touch. "Yes." She sighed, closing her eyes.

"The Elders are waiting," he spoke telepathically.

Cat took another deep breath before exhaling slowly. *"I'm ready."*

He held her face in both hands. *"You can do this, Catriona."*

"You'll be sitting behind me again?"

Heron's gaze gave her the added confidence she needed.

"Directly behind you. I will help you with my thoughts, but whatever you do..."

"I know... I know... do not respond or ask you questions."

"You cannot respond to anything I say, are we clear?"

"Oh lord, Heron... please stop preaching." She smiled. *"If you're sitting behind me, does that mean — ?"*

"Yes, I've got your back."

She pretended not to hear him.

Heron chuckled. *"Good, girl."*

The two gracefully descended the stairs into the Cathedral. The Elders gasped in surprise. It had only been a few days since they had last seen her, but the transformation must have been shocking. She must look like the goddess they had known before her incarnation. The immortal Catriona had emerged.

Heron escorted her to the crimson velvet chair while the Elders nodded respectfully at her. Even Brogan signaled his approval.

"Good day," Brogan announced.

"Good day to you, too," Catriona replied, taking her seat.

Cat exchanged glances with Maeve, who was crossing her fingers in her lap as if hoping the unpleasantness was all behind them. Rhys reached for Maeve's hand and kissed it before cradling it in his own.

Heron, who was standing in front of her, coughed to get her attention. With a twinkle in his eye, he raised his eyebrow in a knowing expression before turning around, bowing to the Elders, and taking his seat behind her

The Elders appeared anxious. None of them enjoyed this process, especially since it involved one of their own. Making little eye contact with one another, they shifted in their seats.

Brogan turned to speak to the group. "Let it be noted we are resuming the Questioning."

He then looked at Heron. Some communication went on between the two before Brogan turned to the Elders. A calm swept over the group.

Brogan's features mellowed. "Let us begin." When he stood directly in front of Cat, she was surprised at the halo of colors surrounding his body. Where was it coming from? She'd never seen him this way before, but she could instantly recognize Brogan's energy in the illuminating colors encircling him. Small waves of shimmering misty light, in violet, blue and gold, pulsed around his divine body.

"May I say, you are looking quite well, Catriona. I trust your three days of relaxation benefited you?"

"It was very relaxing," she said, looking at the rippling energy around the other elders. Why had she not seen this before?

"Are you all right?" Brogan asked.

"*Relax,*" Heron interrupted. "*You are starting to see the living force around objects... beyond their physical form. It is their energy signature."*

Brogan leaned forward. "What is wrong, Catriona?"

"Pretend you do not see anything!" said Heron.

Colorful halos surrounded everything, including the pillars and windows. She looked over at the Elders and saw swirls of blue, gold, and violet spiking out like flames from their bodies. When she looked away, the blur from each color smeared across her line of sight, as if they had been burned into her corneas. Cat quickly shut her eyes, overwhelmed by the phenomenon.

"Do not let on, Catriona!" Heron warned again.

She blinked for several seconds and swallowed hard. "I'm fine."

For the first time, she understood. All living and inanimate objects were not dense, physical things, but matter with a life force around them. Cat felt as if she had been blind and was now able to see for the first time. The experience humbled her.

Brogan shifted his gaze to Heron then looked away.

"Catriona, are you all right?" he asked her.

She nodded.

Heron exhaled loudly.

"I asked this question before, and so I ask it again. What do you fear?"

She collected herself, gearing up to speak, but she mumbled only a few words.

"What?" Brogan asked.

"I'm afraid of the unknown."

Brogan's stood silent, making her wonder if he was thinking of a way to trap her again. He spun around. "And what is the unknown?"

Relief washed over her. She realized she'd been holding her breath. Inhaling deeply, Cat focused her mind. "The unknown is a lack of understanding. What I don't understand, I fear and what I can't control, I fear. I suppose it's basic human behavior."

He grinned. "Well put. So, what can you do about it?"

Something distracted her.

More tiny rainbows of light, like the one that had landed on her hand the first day of the Questioning, floated around the Cathedral. As before, she dismissed them as sunlight reflected through the crystal windows, but this time something more remarkable happened. Each ray of rainbow light appeared to be a small being, alive and dancing about.

"They are happy souls, are they not?" Brogan commented.

"What?" Cat was not sure if she should acknowledge them.

"The lights... they are souls. They come to the Cathedral for communion, to feed off the Elders' positive energy. And, I believe many more came today to see you."

Catriona watched one land beside her on the velvet chair. As she reached toward it, the colorful light jumped in her hand. She raised it to look at it more closely and could clearly feel its thoughts. It was welcoming her back. Cat smiled at it before the little being floated away.

Brogan waited patiently. "I need your attention."

"Oh, yes... right." I suppose the only thing I can do about my fear is to accept there are many things I don't understand and, worse, I can't control."

"Interesting, but can you detach yourself when every cell in your body is telling you to fight or flee? It's a biological response for survival in every human being."

Cat thought a moment. "I guess it depends on the human being. For me, faith in something more intelligent comes into play. That's what I believe when I can't get around it."

He smirked. "There is no other way around it." He walked behind her and leaned over, inches from her ear. "But if I put you back in the Stones, would you figure out another way?"

Her body quaked. The thought of being put back in the hellish pit nearly threw her into a tailspin, but she calmly collected her thoughts. His veiled threat was meant to evoke a reaction of fear, and Cat wasn't giving it to him.

The trepidation began leaving her body with each measured breath. "If that is where you want me to go, Brogan, then fine," she said dryly. "We both realize it's redundant and won't make a bit of difference. I can only control my responses… I can't control what triggers it."

His laugh echoed through the Cathedral. "Another trip into the void will not do the trick either? Are you sure? You came out of it more enlightened the last two times. Maybe the third time is a charm."

"As I said... the decision is yours."

He walked toward the Elders. "What say you? Should we put her back in the Stones?"

They smiled at Cat.

Brogan didn't want to give up easily. "If I understand you correctly, dear Catriona, you are saying you may indeed be afraid, but how you respond to it is the more important factor, correct?"

She nodded.

He walked over and touched her shoulder. "You are learning." He looked at Cat, and his brown eyes twinkled.

Even though Heron was sitting behind her, she sensed he was smiling.

"Now," Brogan continued, "often people will respond to fear with anger, and anger is an enormous issue for you. It is harder for you to deal with than fear will ever be."

Cat looked at the Elders. This emotion had been her downfall more times than could be counted. Anger was her "go to" emotion. She didn't want to be angry, but sometimes a good shout with a few cuss words thrown in was needed. Just like popping a valve on a pressure cooker, she just needed to release some pent-up rage every now and again.

As a counselor, Catriona had taught others to express anger in a constructive, non-threatening way. She believed unexpressed anger ruined a person's mental health and affected them physically. She'd seen too many clients with high blood pressure and heart problems due to repressed rage.

"Hmm... seems I touched a nerve with that question," Brogan said.

"Yes." Catriona spoke up. "I get angry, but only with good reason. What does my fear and anger have to do with helping Earth?"

"You do not suppose these two emotions have any impact on humanity?"

She shrugged. "Yes, they have an impact on humanity, but what does it have to do with me? I'm human, too. Are you saying it's bad?"

"Not at all. Both emotions are helpful if controlled. Otherwise, they can run rampant, causing chaos and destruction in their wake. When that happens it involves many people, even if the emotion was initially only felt by one person."

"It's about perception?" she asked.

"Yes. It is all about perception. Whenever you see a perceived injustice, what do you do?"

"Get angry," she replied.

"Do you believe anger is a positive or negative response?"

"It depends."

"Depends on what?"

Cat tipped her head to the side. "Some anger is justifiable, and some anger is not."

"Explain the difference." Brogan asked.

"Well, I think there are people who are grumpy and angry all the time. Nothing particular triggers them, they are who they are, and are angry for no apparent reason. Then you have those who get upset when something is unbalanced or not fair. You see, Brogan, anger used in a positive manner expresses a desire for change."

"It needs to be justifiable, then, to be all right?" he asked.

Cat nodded.

Brogan snatched one of the tiny rainbows out of the air and smashed his hands together. "I squeezed the life out of this innocent being, for no reason. How does that make you feel?"

"Why would you do that!?" she snapped.

How could he be so cruel to an innocent soul? If a theme had run consistently through Cat's life, it was her sense of justice. She always defended those who were weaker and unable to stand up for themselves: the innocents, the oppressed, and the bullied. Cat would never think twice, sometimes making it a mission to verbally take down the oppressors. Vengeance had become her middle name. Watching Brogan's apathy toward the little light-being appalled her.

"Wait," he said, "your response now... is it a positive response or a negative one?"

She clenched her teeth. "My reaction was justifiable."

"Exactly, and humanity has not learned the difference yet. *If* they had, there would not be so much imbalance." The Council Leader opened his palms, and the unharmed colorful ray of light hovered a moment before drifting away. "I am trying to explain I do not believe, as an Observer, you have any control over that emotion."

"There is a difference. I don't become angry for no reason."

Brogan stood in front of her. "It does not matter. Anger is anger."

"I disagree."

"Stop! Listen to his words, Catriona," Heron pleaded.

She wrinkled her face.

"Catriona," the Council Leader explained, "Please try to understand, anger for a human is normal, but not for an Observer... you must accept it, whatever form it is in."

She looked down.

Brogan walked over and tilted her chin to meet his gaze. "Anger will bring you to tears, but there is no place for it here. Believe me when I say the Brotherhood will focus on that emotion more than any other. They will break you with it. If you cannot contain it, you do not stand a chance."

Sixteen

Ruarc stood in the clearing on the outskirts of the Thirteenth Realm, known as the Fortress of Shadows. He had been banished by the Elders when he and Brogan disagreed upon matters pertaining to Earth. When the gods had split into two groups, Ruarc's followers had stood by him claiming he was the only true god.

He liked being known as "the menacing one" and exercised brute leadership upon his immortal followers. Even though they were referred to as the Brotherhood, Ruarc described all of them as "minions" and reveled in their misery, and the misery of the other souls trapped in the Fortress. Ruarc was amused by the stories that characterized him as evil, and he felt honored the citizens of the earthly realm had written versions of him in their books.

Ruarc was not a patient god. If, at any point, he was displeased he simply "reassigned" his followers to perform dull tasks within the Fortress, rather than participating in the operation of the universe. They could voice alternatives, but not argue with him. Unlike the Council of Elders, the Brotherhood was no democracy.

Balfour had given Ruarc a full report after seeing Catriona with Heron at the Blue Crystal Towers. It had been his mission to spy on her from the second she entered the Thirteenth Realm, but lately, he had nothing new to share. Every day Balfour wandered to the other side waiting patiently for any sign of her, but there were none. He found it strange she didn't leave the

Elder Temple.

When Balfour was sent to inquire about the Observer again, he was met with the excuse that she had not acclimated well to the realm and needed more time. This appeared suspicious to the Brotherhood, considering most Observers didn't have a problem transitioning over.

Balfour returned to Ruarc, who mulled over the news, wondering why certain protocols weren't being followed. As was customary, the Observer was housed on the other side with the Elders. Ruarc hadn't heard a formal announcement of her arrival. What was the secrecy all about? It wasn't normal for him to be the one slighted.

Normally, the Questioning transpired because of a request by the Elders. But since Source had implemented the Shift, Ruarc had initiated the Questioning process.

The Shift might make it harder for Ruarc, as the leader of the Brotherhood, to influence humanity. It appeared to favor the Elders, but he knew he couldn't argue, for he and the Elders were equally helpless against Source. Before he could tip the scales in the Brotherhood's favor, correcting the imbalance, formal measures must be executed.

It was the same routine, over and over again, like two children complaining to their parents the other had gotten more candy. The only consistency during all these Questionings had been Ruarc's power over each Observer. If he could manipulate them, any decisions he deemed favorable to the Elders could be watered down.

"They are all assembled." Balfour's voice resounded from behind him.

"Good," Ruarc headed toward the Shadow Temple to meet with the others.

When he strode into the halls of the Fortress, everyone bowed. His commanding qualities, above all else, bought their loyalty.

Ruarc walked into the throne room. "This Observer, something is wrong."

He plopped himself down in the comfortable golden seat, ornate with precious diamonds and the finest red silk. The rest of the Brotherhood sat below him at a long sturdy iron table.

The minions of the Brotherhood talked amongst themselves.

"Am I invisible?" Ruarc shouted.

They looked up. "No, Sir."

He looked at Balfour. "Explain to me again your findings. When's the last time you were able to see her?"

"On the day she arrived, Sir," he replied.

Ruarc rolled his eyes at him. "Tell me exactly what you saw."

Balfour cleared his throat. "I followed the Observer and one of the Elders from the Temple early that day. He appeared to be giving her a tour."

Ruarc nodded. "Go on. Did she appear ill at all?"

"No, Sir. She looked overwhelmed, but nothing out of the ordinary. At one point she was rolling around in the grass, laughing. She seemed fine after a while. They looked cozy."

"What do you mean by 'cozy'?"

"Well, Sir, she seemed happy to be in the Thirteenth Realm, as Observers usually are. I got the impression they were comfortable with one another. They walked around, not talking much. He even gave her a little cuddle."

"A cuddle? Where was her Guide the whole time?"

"I don't know. The Elder was the only one I saw with her."

Ruarc rubbed his chin. "That's not a protocol. Why would an Elder be parading an Observer around? Go back to the Elder Temple and demand to see her. Make sure they understand I want confirmation she is there."

"Yes, Sir." Balfour got up to leave.

"Wait!" Ruarc raised his hand. "Never mind... I'm coming with you. I want to speak with Brogan myself."

Ruarc and Balfour left the Fortress and traveled to the Thirteenth Realm toward the Elder Temple. When they reached its borders, the faces of its occupants twisted in confusion when they eyed the two gods walking around in their territory. This wasn't a common sight. Only when a pressing issue presented itself did the Brotherhood's presence in the Realm matter. It must be important.

Strolling up the wide marble steps to the front of the Roman inspired building, Ruarc pulled the bell cord. A woman dressed in dark green clothing slowly opened the door. Her eyes widened at the sight of them.

"Welcome. Who are you here to see?"

"I want to see Brogan immediately."

"Come in."

Pushing past her, Ruarc blazed his way into the long vestibule filled with glistening light. Long marble pillars adorned each side of the expansive corridor. A red carpet runner extended from the front door all the way to the Cathedral entrance. Images carved in glowing gemstones graced the hallway, along with gold and silver statues. Every corner of the foyer was bathed in the sunlight.

Ruarc covered his eyes. "It's always too damn bright in here."

When they reached the Cathedral, the woman abruptly turned around, halting them. "Wait!" she said. "I will need to announce your visit. Please stay here." Her look warned them not to enter. Leaving Ruarc and Balfour, she entered the Cathedral, closing the large white doors behind her.

"Hasn't changed much," Ruarc said.

"Does it ever bother you that you left?" Balfour asked.

"Why would it? I don't belong here. The Shadow Temple is far grander than this."

Balfour nodded.

Ruarc laughed. "There's nothing here but a bunch of fools roaming these halls."

"I agree with you there, Sir."

Ruarc touched one of the sculptures. "Why must we keep going through these Questionings? If they'd listen to logic, there would be no reason to bring an Observer here in the first place."

"Pardon me for saying, Sir, but you're the one who called for the Questioning this time."

Ruarc glared at him. "Yes, I am aware, but it's still a colossal waste," he sighed, gesturing around the room. "And yet, here we are."

"It seems you are more concerned about this Observer than the ones in the past. Why is it so important for us to see Brogan this time?"

"My senses are telling me they are hiding something. I'm taking measures to be certain that is not the case."

The woman opened the large doors. "You may speak with him, but understand this is a professional visit, and only out of courtesy are you being allowed to enter."

The leader of the Brotherhood rudely glared at her while she ushered them in.

Brogan stood in the center of the room, surrounded by the other Elders. They seemed to be scrutinizing their guests. Heron moved closer to Cat.

"Am I interrupting?" Ruarc asked, while he and Balfour walked down the shiny marble stairs.

Cat sat in a beautifully engraved chair in the middle of the

Cathedral, but her back was to him.

"Good day, Ruarc. What could possibly drag you away from the Fortress of Shadows to come visit us here on this beautiful day?" Brogan said.

"I want a word with you."

"First, let me do some introductions. This is Catriona, the Observer."

Cat had been warned, moments before, that members of the Brotherhood had come to visit and instructed to stay calm. She turned toward the guests, preparing herself for a hideous sight. Dressed in a white button-down shirt, with the sleeves rolled up, and black pants that fit perfectly over his lean muscular build was a strikingly attractive immortal. He had an earthy, rustic appearance. Cat's breath caught in her throat when Ruarc kissed her hand. His sexy jade eyes pierced through her.

"Hello, Catriona. I am Ruarc. God and leader of the Brotherhood."

Cat smiled graciously. He wasn't some ugly ogre as she had imagined, quite the opposite. He was truly handsome with dark blonde hair pulled into a short ponytail. His skin was perfect. He had a symmetrical face with a square jawline and high cheekbones. All kinds of colors swirled around his aura: crimson, orange, and a little gold and violet. Although Ruarc oozed sensual energy, she could sense the danger lurking behind his facade.

Ruarc paused. "Well, I came to check on the welfare of our lovely guest. We were surprised no announcements had been made and thought a visit was in order."

Brogan approached him. "That is understandable. Unfortunately, Catriona felt ill after her transition, which forced us to allow her to rest a few days prior to the Questioning."

"Oh, yes... about that. I have a request. Would it be possible for the Brotherhood to start it this time? Since there are no hard and fast rules, I thought it only fair. The Council of Elders always seems to get the first shot at the Observers."

"I am sorry, but we already began," Brogan said.

"You should have officially sent notification regardless," Ruarc said. "We are all to be a part of the festivities which mark an Observer's arrival. How long has she been here, a week?"

"No, not quite that long," Brogan said.

Ruarc turned to Cat. "I'm sorry to hear you weren't feeling well, but you look radiant now. The Thirteenth Realm seems to be agreeing with you."

Cat nodded. "Thank you."

"And I apologize for the lack of communication, but we figured you already knew she had arrived, as is usually the case," Brogan said.

"True." Ruarc smiled. "But it is the modus operandi, if for no other reason than to be polite."

"Well, it is good you visited, Ruarc. We are doing things backwards, but only because we did not want Catriona to be ill for the festivities. She needed some time to adjust."

Ruarc turned to Catriona, dipping his head. "Then by all means, continue on. After you're finished, she will come to the Fortress of Shadows as my guest."

Brogan nodded.

"I won't keep you from your task. No reason for dragging this on longer than necessary. That'll only delay our time together." Ruarc rubbed Cat's hands in his before kissing them again. "I'm looking forward to your company."

Heron stood behind Brogan, clenching his jaw.

Cat was taken aback. She didn't know what to say. Part of her faced certain death, and the other part enjoyed it.

Heron interrupted her thoughts. *"He is dangerous, Catriona. You must never misjudge him. EVER!"*

"Until then," she said politely.

Ruarc turned to leave. "By the way, where is your Guide?"

Cat glanced at Brogan, not sure what to say.

"I am her Guide." Heron moved toward Ruarc.

The two gods stood, eyeing one another. There was obvious friction. Cat wondered how far back their rivalry went.

Ruarc arched his brow. "An Observer with an Elder as a Guide? Interesting. I recall Elders who directly assisted in the past, but that was eons ago... before certain rules."

"What rules?" Heron said. "Source requires Observers to have Guides as well. Being an Elder in service is acceptable. As gods, we may assist by undertaking various roles within our creations."

"I am well aware of assisting others in our creations," Ruarc said softly, looking at Catriona.

Cat's face felt hot, and she looked down.

Ruarc smiled and turned back to Brogan. "It is odd an Elder would volunteer to do such a boring task. Were all the other Guides taken?"

The Council Leader stood between the other two gods. "What are you implying, Ruarc? We have all been monitoring potential Observers. When the list of candidates was narrowed down, you agreed to choose Catriona as well."

"You are right. I agreed. I did not realize her Guide was one of yours."

"And that makes a difference, how?" Brogan replied.

Ruarc flashed a grin at him. "It doesn't. He must abide by certain limitations and not interfere with her choices... it's Universal Law. If he does, there are consequences."

Brogan nodded. "Exactly."

"Well, have a pleasant day." Ruarc looked at Cat. "Try not

to keep her too long. I'm looking forward to this beautiful creature's company."

Catriona tried to avoid his gaze. What was he doing to her? His manner was strong and self-assured, and the way he carried his body was hypnotic. She was troubled to think he could easily affect her. Sexy in every sense of the word, Ruarc was one immortal she must be wary of.

Ruarc motioned to Balfour, and the pair strolled out.

Brogan looked at Cat. "He is what I warned you about. Let us all take a short break."

They all exited the Cathedral except Heron, who glared at Cat.

"Are you easy?"

"Excuse me?"

"You practically swooned. Did you enjoy his attention?"

"Oh, please. I was only being polite."

"Do not be, not around him! You must be on your guard, Catriona. His words will make you warm and fuzzy inside, and in the next second, you will be down on your knees, scared and confused."

"Kind of like what happened when I met you?"

Heron sighed. "This is his way of checking on you. After witnessing your reaction, he will assume he is a crow with easy pickings. His game is to lure you in. That is what he does."

"I'm sorry, I was taken off guard. I expected a demon with horns or something,"

"Yes, you were. Immortals can shift into anything we like. I have seen Ruarc in other forms much less attractive."

Heron hugged Cat. "Do not worry--we will not let you leave the Elder Temple until you are ready."

"Okay," she mumbled.

Brogan approached them and touched Cat's shoulder,

"There is work to do, you two. Let us get back to it, shall we?"

Seventeen

Catriona slouched in the velvet cushioned chair and played with the trimming on her dress, thinking she should have been better prepared. She tried not to imagine what awaited her when she was in the Brotherhood's grip. Ruarc had seen how easily he could push her buttons. *Ruarc is a dangerous immortal, devious and deceitful with the poisonous charm of a snake.*

"Are we ready to resume?" Brogan asked.

The compassion and understanding in his eyes centered her. "Yes," she replied.

"Living an earthly life is interesting, no doubt. You have seen all sides of human nature. Some you have directly experienced, and others through observation. Given the current circumstances, where do you suppose mankind is headed?"

Cat looked over at the Elders. "I don't know. Some days I feel good about humanity, and other days I'm sickened at what I see. Man is fickle."

"Go on," Brogan prompted.

"Children are like clay, being molded by both our parents and society, taught to think or act a certain way. As children, we're brought into this world with such high expectations, both from our parents and for ourselves. The boundary between right and wrong gets confused when we're told not to do something, but see others doing it. The lines are often blurred."

He nodded. "So people are in a constant state of conflict?"

"In one form or another, yes. Either a direct conflict or a

moral one."

Brogan began pacing. "Does this disappoint you?"

"Yes, it's sad to see a pure soul corrupted by its environment. Humans are like pack animals who want to run with others of the same outlook and mindset. At the same time, we are spiritual beings. It's a duality. I wish all of humanity would evolve."

"Good answer." Heron silently beamed, causing Catriona to smile.

"Would you say humanity is inferior?" Brogan continued.

She paused. "Compared to whom? The inferiority is by design. Humanity has as many good qualities as bad. I think most strive for goodness but are tempted, through circumstances or desperation, to act in ways they normally wouldn't. Sometimes negative influences prompt them to do evil through a sense of self-preservation."

"Do you believe their downfall is from a lack of wisdom, then?"

"No. It's from a deliberate suppression of wisdom."

"How do you know if mankind was meant to be any more than what it already is?"

She giggled. "Well, if this is the best you gods can do, then I'm disappointed."

He clasped his hands behind his back. "Mankind is, at the least, flawed, but you know why that is, do you not?"

She nodded. "It seems we are caught in a tug-of-war."

"Definitely. We have such high hopes. You have not seen anything yet. Do you believe an intervention is in order?"

Cat considered his remark. "Only if it involves an evolution of consciousness. Man needs to mature into the potential beings we were meant to be. People who think and act for the best possible outcome for all involved... not just the outcome for ourselves. And it would be much nicer if we weren't negatively influenced."

Heron gave her a mental high five.

After several more hours of questioning, Brogan called for a recess to allow Catriona to rest. Heron escorted her back to her chambers, making sure more food was brought to her and she ate enough to keep her strength.

Something in his manner suggested he was concerned. About what, he wouldn't let on, but Catriona knew better.

"What is troubling you?" She finished the rest of the wine in her glass.

He grinned at her. "Nothing. You did well today."

"Thank you," she said, still eyeing him. Heron stared off in the distance not saying a word.

After a few minutes, Catriona could take no more silence. "What is your problem? I told you I was sorry about my behavior earlier."

"No, it is not that," he replied.

She sat down and patted the seat beside her. He reluctantly walked over. "Don't tell me you were jealous?"

"What? No."

She treaded lightly. "Ruarc genuinely irritates you, why?"

"Who does he not irritate? The Elders and the Brotherhood do not get along, in case you did not figure that out."

Catriona placed her hand on his arm. "I see many things, like how tense you got as soon as he walked into the room." She squeezed his bicep. "See, you're still tense." She began massaging his shoulders.

Heron sat there enjoying her touch. "To be honest, Ruarc and I share a history."

"What kind of history?"

"Let us say, we do not get along... leave it at that."

"But I can't," she replied.

Heron wrestled with his thoughts which, fortunately, Catriona was deaf to. He wanted to explain further, but he knew if he told her, she'd run from the room screaming in terror. If the Stones were bad, wait until the Brotherhood had her. By the time they were done, it would make her treatment at the Elder Temple seem like an amusement park.

"You will understand once you start the Questioning with them. I advise you to be watchful and alert."

"I will."

He snatched her hand. "All I can say is Ruarc may appear to be a gentleman, but he is not. He'll find your weaknesses. Do not be the fly."

"What do you mean?"

"A spider lures its victims with a beautiful sticky web. An insect does not see it until it is too late, but by then the spider is upon it, spinning the sticky thread around it until it is all wrapped up. The spider may not eat its victim right away, so it is incapacitated until its captor decides to bite. Ruarc is like that, Catriona. He may leave you there for a while, awake, helpless and afraid, before coming back to finish you off."

Cat shuddered. "That's a horrible analogy."

Heron shrugged his shoulders. "It is true."

"All right. You're my Advisor. What would you have me do?"

"Do not get drawn in... he is not to be trusted, at all. You may find him charming, but it is all a front."

"Do you think I wanted his attention?"

"Did you not?"

"I couldn't help my response, but now I'll be more cautious. Ruarc's dangerous, I can sense it a mile away. I'll exercise my integrity."

"Well, exercise harder. He will test you at every turn."

She gave him a reassuring peck on the cheek. "But you'll be there with me, right, keeping me safe? You have my best interests at heart."

"I do. Now, let us get out of here. Come take a walk with me." Heron offered his hand.

"Can I?"

"With the exception of the terrace, you have not been outside since the first day you arrived. It is time to get more sunlight on that pretty face of yours."

"A wonderful idea."

Cat enjoyed being outside, and walking around in the beauty of nature, with Heron beside her, lifted her mood. All the energy within the Thirteenth Realm fed her soul with much needed peace. She could easily get lost anywhere and not care. The day was indescribable, as pristine as she remembered from her first day there. Seeing everything surrounded by its energy signature took a while to get used to. It was like truly seeing for the first time. Objects appeared in lighter form, and a halo of colors radiated around them and passed through them.

The leisurely stroll allowed Cat to consider her internal rhythm, which seemed to fade with each passing second. Her mind and body adapted to whatever cycle of day presented itself. Being completely in the "now," Catriona had a sense of liberation, allowing things to unfold naturally without forcing any expectations.

They passed a lilac bush that filled the air with a pungent, sweet odor. Cat buried her nose in one of the stems, taking in full breaths and sighing at its delightful, heady aroma. Heron plucked off a couple of bunches and handed them to her to hold on their journey.

People they passed on the streets smiled, greeting them with nods and occasional hellos. Everyone was dressed in the colorful attire designating their professions. It finally occurred to her everyone had a reason for being there. Nothing was random. Each person was a puzzle piece that fit perfectly into the whole, for the whole cannot function without all of the pieces.

Strolling past buildings with unique architecture, Catriona noticed more details than before, pausing at each place to ask Heron about its purpose. He explained their function and how crucial each was in the scheme of the realm. The organization and efficiency amazed her. Everything gave off such vibrant energy--words alone could not describe it.

This is home. The words echoed in her mind. This is what she had missed on Earth. Her immortal side longed for its return to paradise, a freedom from the chaotic energies surrounding her. Maybe this is death, and it was beautiful.

Before long, they found themselves standing at the Blue Crystal Towers. It was a landmark for the Thirteenth Realm, a beacon of healing and hope. Catriona caught her breath, once again, staring at its towering magnificence. Words could not describe the loving energy. Sunlight shimmered through the structure, fracturing light into a rainbow spectrum streaming in all directions.

Heron turned to her. "I debated bringing you here, but I wanted you to see it. The miracles performed within these Towers come from the most revered and powerful immortal healers in the entire universe."

She stood there, listening to the Towers call to her, but all she could do was watch in yearning while she touched the smoothness of its walls.

Heron grasped Cat's hand. "Do you want to go inside?"

She looked at him in surprise. "Yes... yes, I do."

They walked past the long reflecting pool and the water

fountain to the main entrance. He threw open the double doors and bowed to her. "My lady, after you."

Catriona shivered when she entered the foyer. Being inside evoked such a strong emotion of longing. Her eyes began to mist.

Standing before them was a garden atrium with a humungous waterfall off to the right. The waterfall jutted out of the wall, flowing into to a pond full of lilies and various plants. The calming, tropical atmosphere and the sound of the falling water provided a soothing ambiance with white noise in the background.

Exotic birds of brilliant colors flew around, squawking. Some were preening themselves on branches. One flew inches from Cat's head before landing on a rock beside her.

She looked up and was amazed to find the middle part of the Towers was hollow in the center. One could peer all the way to the sky. No wonder the light appeared to go straight through it. Elevators and small walkways with railings looped around the interior, giving access to the other two towers and the floors above.

Cat was compelled to figure out where to go next.

She strolled across a huge wooden bridge. Coral-colored fish shimmered in the pond below. They rose to the surface and their huge mouths opened and closed as if to greet her. She paused, looking down, laughing at them for a few seconds before crossing completely over.

Once on the other side, Catriona instinctively sensed where she was going and chose to take a certain walkway that ascended to the left. She was so driven to explore that Heron had to double his pace to keep up with her. Following a compulsion, she climbed higher and higher on the graded path, until she arrived at one of the upper levels.

Looking back at her Advisor, she stopped. "This is the floor where I work," she said, in a matter-of-fact tone. Heron gave her a knowing grin. By now, Cat appeared fully aware of her surroundings. Walking down the hallway, she spied a particular door. She stood in front of it and froze.

"What is wrong?" Heron whispered.

She swallowed hard. "Nothing."

"Catriona?" he asked.

"I'm fine." A smile curved her lips. "I'm remembering bits and pieces now."

Catriona slowly turned the doorknob on the shaded glass door and peeked inside. As the pair entered, the large room came alive, bursting with bright intensity. Cat had to shield her eyes with her arm. "I remember," she said.

"Remember what?" he asked. He couldn't see either.

She moved cautiously around the space until she found the switch on the wall that lowered the blinds. The room continued pulsing with a strong energy that bounced off the walls as if it were aware of her return and happy to see her.

Cat giggled. "This is my healing room."

Eighteen

Ruarc sat on his golden throne in the Shadow Temple, his private domain, and sipped red wine out of a sparkling bejeweled chalice. The scent of the dry brew hung heavy in his nostrils while he savored the oak aroma on his tongue. He stopped to rub the cool vessel against his forehead, contemplating the events of the day.

The large creaking double doors opened into the lavishly decorated room. Balfour stumbled in, obviously imbibing on the wine himself, and walked up the lush green runner that led to his Master. The silver wine carafe engraved with symbols overflowed, spilling wine between his hands.

Master, Balfour thought with disdain as he neared the throne. Out of all the Brotherhood, Balfour was the one Ruarc trusted most. It was only because he had stood by Ruarc when he instigated the mutiny that had split the gods into two groups. Although Balfour was equal in terms of power, Source had granted Ruarc the title of Leader, giving Balfour the task of being second in command. Calling him "Sir" and "Master" was degrading, but it was what Source demanded, after the separation, to maintain balance, and they all must fall in line or face consequences.

Standing before Ruarc, Balfour offered to fill his drink, noticing his disgruntled expression.

"Something troubles you, Sir?" Balfour asked.

Ruarc held out the chalice, looking down at him. "Did you see how the Elders acted?"

Balfour nodded. "Yes, I did."

Ruarc stood up. "What do you suppose they're hiding? Do they believe I'm an idiot? I am a god. They can't hide anything from me."

Balfour shrugged. "They know we're always watching, Sir. What could they possibly hide?"

"Good question. Brogan should've been more annoyed at our unexpected visit, but they were calm and guarded." He took a gulp of wine. "There's something else going on. I can feel it."

"Yes, Sir."

Ruarc swished the heady drink back and forth in his chalice. "I can't put my finger on it yet, but I will." He guzzled the rest of the wine and held it out to Balfour.

The subordinate filled the chalice to the top. "Maybe the Elders are protective because they know how we treat Observers."

His comment evoked a laugh. "Do my techniques leave something to be desired?" asked Ruarc.

"You're definitely cruel," Balfour replied, drinking from the carafe. The red liquid dribbled from the corners of his mouth onto the green runner.

The menacing one frowned at him. "And?"

"What I mean is--"

"I don't give a damn what you mean," interrupted Ruarc. "And stop drinking my wine! It makes you messy and spineless."

"Yes, Master."

"I don't want Observers being too comfortable."

"No, Sir. We wouldn't want that," Balfour replied.

Ruarc turned and paced around the room. "Something doesn't seem right."

"And what would that be?"

"This Observer, she's different."

"Do you think you're reading too much into this, Sir? They said she was ill."

"Yes, I know. But when I approached her, she had this presence."

Balfour hiccupped. "What do you mean?"

Ruarc walked over to a table with a plate of fresh fruit and picked up a ripe purple grape before plopping it ungracefully into his mouth. "She's different."

"Not to mention she's one of the more beautiful Observers we've had," Balfour responded.

The leader waved his hand dismissively.

"Besides that. There's something mystical about her. A strength and power I have not seen in the Observer species before."

Balfour placed the carafe on the table, scratching his head. "On Earth she's a healer, but many Observers are capable of that function. She seemed normal to me." He shrugged.

Ruarc sat on the throne again and pounded his fist on the arm rest. That's just it... she's not! You've been watching her. Did you notice anything out of the ordinary?"

The subordinate god stood below him. "There were times she knew things, in the intuitive sense, but that's not unusual for an Observer either. May I ask what you're looking for?"

"An angle."

"I believe you might be assuming too much, Sir."

"That's why I am the god of this dominion, and not you!"

Balfour attempted to calm him. "You are a powerful god, and I am at your service. What do you need me to find out?"

The menacing one schemed a moment. "I want to know everything about her, especially why an Elder is her Guide."

"Weren't you a Guide once?"

"Hell no, I'm a god. One would have to be bored out of their skull to even consider it. Here we create, manipulate, and pull the strings on all our puppets. There we'd only be able to --"

"Guide?" Balfour interrupted.

Ruarc scoffed. "Watch them make their own choices... how pathetic."

Balfour paused. "Maybe Heron had to take such a position before he can replace Brogan."

The sound of Heron's name riled him. "Cocky immortal," Ruarc sneered. "Out of all the Elders, it had to be him."

"You have a troubled past with each other," said Balfour.

Ruarc gave Balfour a deathly stare. "And yet you have the gall to bring it up again?" His subordinate glanced down. "We're forbidden to interview Guides, but we can find out his motive for being one."

The minion cleared his throat. "How are you going to do that, Master? I doubt he'll give you any information."

Ruarc took another swig of wine. "Find his weak spot."

"You'll figure a way, I'm sure."

The leader's face lit up. "And I thought of one. To get to Heron, I need to spend time alone with the enchanting Catriona. Tell the others to convene here... NOW!"

"Sir?"

Ruarc licked wine from his lips. "We're having our festival."

Nineteen

Catriona touched every object in the room in a sentimental way. It was if she was discovering something about herself for the first time. The familiar setting vibrated through her core. How wonderful it was to be in a place she belonged.

The room displayed earthly elements of wood, metal, earth, water, and fire. Plants, candles, and a small ornate water fountain decorated the space. Wooden floors, with an area rug here and there, gave it a comfortable feel. She speculated that it had been done deliberately, so that a soul crossing over would be more relaxed in familiar earthly surroundings.

A bookcase with volumes of books and scrolls--in alphabetical order, but in an ancient language--lined one wall. She couldn't read the dialect, but she had an idea what their purpose was. Metal filing cabinets filled with hard copies of charts sat along another wall holding a record of every soul she had ever healed.

The only objects not of an earthly origin were her desk and the hovering healing table she spotted in the center of the room. The half-moon shaped desk, also made of blue crystal, was illuminated from underneath with a digital keyboard projected on it. She walked over and hit one of the keys. A graph and mathematical equations materialized in front of her, like a huge 3D computer screen. With her index finger, she moved the graphs and data around in midair. Swiping it to the right brought in more data, while swiping to the left minimized it.

Cat wandered over to the bookcase and grabbed one of the

scrolls. She untied the strap and unrolled it, focusing on the foreign words. "I wish I could remember how to read these."

"That will take more time," Heron said.

She put the scroll back in place and went over to the healing table. The shiny, cool surface was made out of a strange metallic material that acted like a gentle magnet. The moment she touched it, it took a bit more effort to pry her fingers apart. *Maybe it was to keep troubled souls from rolling off?*

She turned to Heron. "Get on."

"What type of healing do I need today, dear lady?" He probably wondered why Cat thought he needed any healing-- after all, Heron was a god.

"I'm not sure yet, but I plan to fix you right up."

He walked over to the hovering contraption and lay down.

Cat looked around, expecting something else to happen.

"What are you searching for?" he asked.

"I don't know. There's more to this thing... I'm missing something." Cat studied it a moment.

When she swiped her hand across the bottom of the table, a large crystal opened up directly above them. It descended slowly, branching out into a huge cluster of other crystals, and stopped about three feet above Heron's body.

"That's cool." Catriona laughed.

Large, elongated, immovable quartz crystals, about a foot wide, were in the center. Smaller crystals were attached to thin metal arms that could be swung down and adjusted to rest on any part of the body. All healers used these types of instruments.

The custom of applying crystals had long been practiced in the Thirteenth Realm. Each mobile crystal was approximately two inches wide and served a particular healing purpose. The larger crystals were clear, but the smaller ones were all different colors.

The Advisor lay on his back, casually observing the structure hanging above him. "Hmm, this looks confusing."

Cat stared at it. "I use crystals on Earth, too, but *nothing* like this."

"Show me what you know," he said.

She held her hands out, about three inches from his body, and waved them up and down from the top of his head to his feet, scanning for any imbalances. The information came to her intuitively, so she knew what areas to treat. After her assessment, she chose which crystal to use. She pulled down the metal arm with the rose quartz attached to it and placed it directly over his heart. The cold tip touched his chest. With intense concentration, Cat placed her hands on either side of the rose quartz. Heat radiated from her palms, and soon the crystal started pulsing.

Catriona shut her eyes and intuited many things about her Advisor. Spontaneous information flooded her mind as she quietly lingered on the area for several minutes.

"How do you feel?" she asked.

"Fine..."

Cat continued working with it until the crystal stopped pulsing, meaning the area had healed. She hesitated, then pushed the quartz back into the cluster and offered her hand to help pull Heron to a seated position.

"Is everything all right?"

"I used the rose quartz to help balance your heart chakra," she said, looking away.

"Thank you," he said.

Her bottom lip quivered.

"What is wrong?" Heron asked.

She didn't want to look at him. "You're so sad?"

"I am fine, Catriona."

"No, you aren't," she whispered. "I saw everything."

Her Advisor tried to smile at her. "I am sorry it upset you."

"Don't apologize; I should be the one asking for forgiveness."

"Why?" he asked.

"You're so unhappy… it's because of me."

"In what way?"

She stood next to him. "I sensed our connection when we first met in the café. But when you said you were my Advisor, I just thought it was part of your job."

Heron was silent.

"When you showed me your visions, especially the one with us sitting together talking, I started thinking. I've seen Rhys and Maeve together in the Cathedral. It occurred to me that an immortal could have a significant other."

"Why would that upset you?"

Cat walked to the window and peered out. Tears streaked her cheeks. "I've tried ignoring my feelings… tried rationalizing it away, but I understand now, and I can't help how I feel about you."

Her Advisor stood behind her, touching her arm.

"And the longer I'm here, the easier it is to forget my life on Earth." Cat wiped her eyes. "Precious memories of my family are disappearing, and there's not a damn thing I can do about it."

"This is your true home, Catriona."

She turned to him. "I'm being pulled in two different directions, and I'm losing myself, becoming someone entirely different."

"You *are* someone entirely different. Understand that it was never the other way around."

Cat's eyes widened. "Why are you being so insensitive? I had a life... it was real to me!" She pulled away from him. "Before I say what I need to say, I have to know. When I return to Earth to complete this "mission," what happens next?"

Heron looked down.

"Look at me!" she pleaded. "Why is this happening?"

Heron sighed. "Because you chose it."

"Can I go home when I'm done?"

"No," he whispered. "You planned for all of this in your Life Chart. You just do not remember your reasons right now."

She began wailing.

The Advisor snatched her up into his arms. "Shh... It will be all right. You had to figure this out on your own."

Burying her face in his shoulder, she clung to him. "I've hurt you, and so many people."

He was speechless.

"You knew you wouldn't be able to speak with me, or touch me... only stand by like a ghost. And despite all of that, you still wanted to be my Advisor?"

"I could not let you go alone. I care too much."

Instinctively, he turned his head and gently brushed her lips with his.

Catriona welcomed his intrusion, watching the smoky intensity in his eyes. He paused a moment before his lips pursued hers again. Her pulse quickened. Wrapping her fingers through his hair, Cat deepened their kiss.

He held her closer, seductively trailing his lips down her soft neck to the base of her throat. A whirlwind of energy swirled around them, sending scrolls and books flying across the room before crashing to the floor.

His labored breathing against her neck only unraveled Cat

more. She moaned, crushing his face against her breasts.

As he lifted her up, she wrapped her legs around him. Heron brought her down to the floor in a kneeling position. He sought out her lips again and kissed her so feverishly she couldn't breathe.

She gasped and tilted her head up. Moist, hot air tickled his ear, driving him insane with passion. With one hand, the immortal grabbed the fabric of her ruby dress, pulling it upwards, while his other hand freed himself. He laid her tenderly on the wooden floor, and his fingers entered her, probing softly.

Cat threw her head back, quivering with desire.

He hovered patiently... He wanted her, but paused.

She noticed his apprehension. Trapping his hips between her legs, she pulled him toward her, giving him the response he needed.

A husky sound escaped his throat as he entered her. He thrust slowly at first; then he bore himself deeper and deeper in an unbroken rhythm. Heron cupped her face tenderly in his hands and kissed her while she yielded completely. Putting his arm under her hips, he rolled his full weight upon her.

She savored their union, touching skin to skin with no barriers between them, and while he continued plunging into her, a slow wave built deep within.

Sensing her increased desire, Heron buried himself with each thrust. His breathing quickened, and his muscles tensed with the oncoming release. He let out a lustful groan. Cat responded with a small cry and her body peaked, arching herself against him while rippling waves of pleasure coursed through them both.

Like a bolt of golden lightning binding them together, their energies merged. The sensation was so intense, Cat cried out. Never had she experienced such intensity. The feeling of being completely captured and paired with one another was beyond anything she'd felt before, and Catriona willingly lost herself in him. Heron shuddered, with one last thrust, and another throaty groan escaped his lips before he was spent.

Bracing himself above her, Heron gazed at Cat for a moment, then he rolled her on top of him. They both lay there panting with exhaustion. She placed her ear over his heart, listening to the rapid beats. It was the most beautiful sound she'd ever heard. Catriona sighed.

Twenty

Off in the distance, the sun started setting, casting a pastel orange glow that bounced across thin clouds in the misty cobalt sky. The moons were already high above the horizon, faded in a watercolor tone, side by side waiting to shine in full splendor by nightfall.

Catriona awoke to the sound of Heron's steady heartbeat and the feeling of his chest rising and falling. They were still joined together, comfortable and satisfied.

"*Hello,*" he beamed.

She glanced up at him. "*Hello to you.*"

Heron's thumb brushed against her chin. "*I do not want to leave here anymore than you, but we must get back to the Elder Temple.*"

Cat propped herself up on one elbow. "*Was I asleep long?*"

"*Not too long... I hope I did not drain you too much,*" he teased.

"*It'll take a lot more than one go around to wear me out.*"

"*That can be easily arranged.*"

She rolled her eyes at him. "*This changes everything.*"

"I am aware of that. We should get ready."

She broke away from him and stood up. She ran her fingers through her hair, to untangle the knotted chaos, and smoothed down the wrinkles in her ruby-colored dress.

Heron tucked in his shirt and readjusted his pants, throwing glances at Cat with a twinkle in his eyes.

Cat admired him. He still looked dashingly handsome, all disheveled and his hair a mess.

Surveying the room, the couple noted the books and scrolls cluttering up the floor. "Wow… we need to get this cleaned up," Cat said.

"No problem." Heron winked.

He held his hand out, and the items lifted off the ground, hovered a moment, then flew through the air before settling into their proper places.

"Hands-free cleaning?" she asked. "I could have used that while on Earth."

"You can do this, Catriona. It just takes thought and a lot of focus." He waved his hand and a brown book toppled off the shelf. "There, put that back where it belongs."

She imitated him, putting her hand out and thinking about where she wanted it to go. The book floated but fell back to the ground.

"Do it again."

Cat focused, commanding the item to go to its place. It hovered again, higher this time, and within seconds it leapt back onto the bookshelf.

Heron clapped. "Wonderful. See, you do possess these gifts. What matters is the intent behind it."

"When you say 'intent,' do you mean the emotion behind it?"

He shook his head. "No, I mean positive or negative intention."

Cat was confused.

"Positive is putting it back where it belongs. Negative is hitting me in the head with it. Positive intentions yield constructive results, and negative intentions yield destructive results."

She looked at him. The wheels were turning in her mind.

Her Advisor pointed his finger at her. "Oh, no... do not practice *any* of this unless I am around, understand?"

"Understood." She winked at him.

"You better," he warned. "Now let us go."

She smiled inwardly. Cat wasn't about to tell him all of the things she was already capable of doing.

Heron hurriedly escorted Cat out of the Blue Crystal Towers and back into the open air. As they walked in silence, Cat couldn't help noticing how different she felt after what they had shared back in the Towers. She sensed a deeper connection to him after their lovemaking, and it wasn't some fantasy she had conjured up in her mind.

"Heron?" she said.

He stopped and turned to her.

"What happened between us back at the Towers?"

The immortal smiled at her. "We had an energy exchange."

"What is that?"

He tried to explain. "Um... sex was meant to be more than just a physical connection. It was also supposed to be spiritual. When two come together as one, they exchange energy with one another. It is their essence, something that happens from pure love and is not tainted in any way."

"I've experienced intimate, loving sex before, but never felt anything like that."

"Humans are jaded. Selfishness, jealousy, and perversion, among a myriad of other reasons, prevent this expression."

Heron reached for her hand. "The energy is stagnant and cannot be released properly. Only from a perspective of pure love can it be given and received, yet few truly understand what it is."

"Were humans ever able to accomplish this?"

"Yes, before the Brotherhood corrupted it. Sex, by design, was meant to be more than just physical."

She looked down. "Did I give anything back to you?"

Heron seemed to appreciate her thoughtfulness. "No, Catriona. I gave it to you, but soon you will be able to give it back."

They continued walking.

She felt honored he wanted to share that with her. *Can this immortal be any more endearing?* Catriona was lost on Cloud Nine. Her affection for Heron made her heart expand so much in her chest, at any second she thought it would burst.

"I love you," she beamed toward Heron.

"And I love you," he replied.

Before long, they were already walking up the stairs to the Elder Temple. Cat found it confusing, considering all the time it had taken for them to get to the Towers.

"How did we get back so fast?" she asked. "It took forever the last time."

Heron was already several steps ahead. "I had to stretch your human concept of time a little before returning to the Temple."

"You can do that?"

"Of course."

"You never cease to amaze me." She shook her head, realizing there was much to understand about these immortals. "When will I learn more?"

"In actuality, you do not need to learn anything. You just need to remember how to do it. But in mortal flesh, you are limited.

"How limited?"

"Only a quarter of your divinity is housed in mortal form."

Cat shrugged. "Telepathy and moving objects around is pretty amazing for only a quarter."

"Yes, but…" He smiled. "Imagine what you can do when you are completely immortal, using the other three quarters. Bending time is one of them."

She silently put it on her mental "to do" list and grinned like a Cheshire cat.

When they entered the Elder Temple, Rhys came down the corridor toward them. His cheerful smile greeted them. "Good day."

"Good day, Rhys," Catriona replied.

"Brogan asked, if I ran into either one of you, to guide you both toward the Oval Room. Something of an important nature needs to be discussed."

Heron looked at Catriona, then back at the other Elder. "Is everything all right?"

"I do not know." Rhys rubbed his chin. "I am sure it is nothing of real importance, or we would be out searching for you. By the way, where were you two?"

Heron said nothing.

"Heron was kind enough to let me go outside for a long walk," Cat said.

"You have been indoors quite a bit. It is probably the best thing he could have done."

Cat and Heron avoided looking at each other.

"Well, I must go," Rhys said. "I hope to see you again soon, Catriona."

"Me too, Rhys."

Rhys grabbed Catriona's hand and kissed it. "I was impressed with you today during the Questioning. Keep up the good work." With a wink, he proceeded on his way.

As they rounded the corner toward the Oval Room, their steps slowed. Still relatively fresh from their union, neither one seemed comfortable facing Brogan.

"Let me do all of the talking," Heron said softly before knocking.

"Come in, please," a voice boomed from inside.

Heron turned to Cat. "Whatever it is, stay calm."

She nodded, and they entered the room, trying to seem nonchalant.

"Take a seat," the Council Leader said. He didn't face them.

The pair glanced at one another. Heron rubbed her shoulder and gave it a firm squeeze before sitting down. He folded his hands on the crystal table.

A deep breath escaped Brogan's lips. "I just received word from Ruarc that he still wishes to host a festival in Catriona's honor."

Cat was stunned.

"As you already heard, it is customary for the Observer to partake in festivities prior to the Questioning. The festival is generally a joint event organized by both the Elders and the Brotherhood, but since we did not plan one, Ruarc has requested we plan it now."

Heron looked at Cat. "I do not think it is necessary at this point... do you?

She shrugged.

"What was your reply?" Heron asked Brogan.

"I told him we would be happy to co-host a festival--"

"No," Heron interrupted.

"Before you refuse remember, Heron, we must deflect any suspicions," said Brogan, sitting next to Cat.

"We should have planned festivities when she first came, to avoid arousing any suspicion in the very beginning," Heron said.

Brogan paused. "Then he could have seen her prior to her transformation, stirring even more suspicion. How would we explain that? They would have seen an older, darker haired woman, still beautiful." He smiled at Catriona. "But not the vibrant being before us now."

Heron thought a moment. "Ah, you are right."

"Excuse me," Catriona asked. "I don't understand. Haven't the Brotherhood been watching me most of my life?"

"Only at certain intervals," said Brogan. "The concern is not that you appear different. The concern is you appear dramatically different. Most Observers do gain a certain amount of vitality in the Thirteenth Realm, but your appearance has altered considerably."

"Hmm, I wonder why," she beamed to Heron, sarcastically.

He shot her a strange look, which luckily went undetected by the Council Leader.

"If they had seen you when you first arrived, and then saw you now, it would raise questions."

Catriona couldn't help herself. "Why do you think that is, Brogan? Why am I so different from other Observers?"

"I told you to let me do all the talking," said Heron.

The Council Leader looked at her with his tender brown eyes. "You are a special soul, my dear. I have grown very fond of you."

"And I of you. But I still know there is something you aren't telling me."

"Do not go there, Catriona!" Heron cautioned.

"Each Observer has a certain type of personality. It is an ability to detach emotionally and stay objective. For some reason, you can be a bit more emotional than most."

Catriona knew he was twisting the intent of her words but wasn't about to press the issue.

"I see such improvement in your ability to carry yourself and, with more practice, you will be able to take on whatever may come your way."

She laughed. "That doesn't sound comforting."

He reached for her hand and held it firmly in his. "You are strong, Catriona. You will make it through the Questioning in one piece, maybe a few scratches and bruises, but still in one piece."

She didn't know if he meant it metaphorically or not, but Cat appreciated his concern. His words were genuine and, for the first time, Catriona felt safer around him, even though he could put her back in the Stones whenever he wished.

"You realize demanding this festival is a ploy," Heron said.

"Of course it is." Brogan tapped the crystal table. "There is no doubt in my mind Ruarc couldn't care less if a festival took place or not. He is annoyed that we dug our heels in this time. There have been occasions, in the past, when there were no festivals, and we heard no rumblings from the Brotherhood at all."

"Why do you think he is being so persistent?" Heron asked.

"My guess is he wants to get familiar with Catriona."

Catriona could sense Heron's blood boiling.

"It is because of me, isn't it?"

"I do not think he is happy knowing a member of the Elders is her Advisor. He will have it out for you, I fear. It will be difficult, especially given your past with Ruarc," said Brogan.

"He can't keep Heron and I apart… can he?" Cat asked.

"Oh no, dear, he cannot."

His response wasn't at all convincing. Cat sensed that Brogan had purposely left out a lot of details. Her stomach flip-flopped.

"Please do not concern yourself with this," said Brogan. "As your Advisor, Heron may accompany you wherever you go while you are in the Thirteenth Realm. That means he will be with you at the Fortress of Shadows as well."

"Are you sure of that?" Cat asked, wrapping a strand of hair around her finger.

He smiled to reassure her. "Yes, I am. You only need to ask Heron to be with you, and he must... regardless of whether Ruarc approves or not. He may intervene at any time. That is the rule."

"When will this festival take place?" Heron asked.

The Council Leader sighed. "For Catriona's perception of time, let us say tomorrow evening. I sent for the Elders so they may begin planning everything, but you and I have a lot to discuss. Will you kindly escort her back to her chambers and return here?"

Heron bowed his head to Brogan. "I certainly will."

He stood and offered Catriona his hand to take her back to her chamber.

The bright moonbeams gently weaved through the skylight, casting a misty glimmer against the halls of the Elder Temple. Catriona looked up at the millions of stars in the sky as they walked back to her chamber. At the door, Heron took her into his arms and kissed her so affectionately it made her knees weak.

"Heron, stop." Cat pushed him away. "What are we going to do?"

He grinned at her. "I am not going to ravish you here in the

Elder Temple--someone would surely find out. But they are too busy planning the festival to worry about us at the moment."

"No, that's not what I mean," she said, mock slapping his face. "I'm talking about Ruarc."

Heron's sapphire eyes pierced hers. "My sweet Catriona. I will not let anything happen to you."

She wrapped her arms around his neck and placed her head against his chest. "I'm afraid."

Holding her close, he felt her trembling in his arms. He kissed the top of her head. "Trust me, I will be with you."

Catriona intuitively believed he'd do everything in his power to protect her, but even immortals have limits, especially when pitted against each other. Doubt was germinating in her mind.

Heron released her. "I must return to the Oval Room. Please get some sleep."

"Until tomorrow?"

"Please do not worry," he said gently. "Sweet dreams to you."

She watched him stride off. Looking back at her, he flashed a bright smile as he rounded the corner, and then he was out of sight. Catriona stood all alone with a heavy, sick sensation aching in her belly. It was the same symptom she'd always gotten when circumstances were about to change for the worse.

Twenty-One

The next morning came so fast Catriona didn't know what had hit her. When her weary eyes opened to the new day, it seemed she had just laid her head on the pillow. She had been awoken by Heron, who had dutifully knocked at her chamber door.

The gnawing ache hadn't left her stomach all night, but she did her best to hide it from her Advisor, who chatted away about the day's events, not seeming to notice her discomfort.

Heron insisted on them speaking, rather than using telepathy, as an added insurance. Cat listened to him patiently. She was annoyed that he insisted on verbal communication, but she understood what was at stake if she slipped and they were caught.

He instructed her on what to expect from the Elders and the Brotherhood during the evening festivities, warning her about Ruarc's potential tactics and how she must stay guarded. Cat was grateful it was only for one night. Then they could put the whole affair behind them... or so she hoped.

After Heron had left her chamber to take care of last minute plans, Cat paced around the room like a caged animal. She had quite a bit of faith in herself but dreaded having to go through the ordeal in the first place. At least Heron would be nearby to run interference should things get too intense.

A wave of fear spurred her to leave her chamber and go for

a walk around the Elder Temple to clear her head. Sneaking out the red door, she peeked both ways, finding it odd the halls always seemed deserted. She walked down the corridors, up the stairwells, and through the foyers, strolling for what seemed like hours. On and on she went, in a daze, until Cat forgot where she was. She started to backtrack but became more confused. Up or down? Left or right? Everything started looking the same, and the funny thing was not another soul passed her, so she couldn't ask for help. Where was everyone?

Catriona turned left onto another hallway. Several doors lined the hall on each side. They appeared to be entrances to more chambers instead of the communal areas of the Elder Temple. Her curiosity got the best of her. She tried each door but discovered they were all locked. She tried knocking.

"Hello, is anyone in here?"

Finding no one, Cat continued her journey down the hallway, and a flicker appeared out of the corner of her eye. She turned around, and a shape emerged in front of her. Staring in awe at the transformation, she recognized the strong, masculine immortal with dark hair and sparkling sapphire eyes looking back at her.

He was so fine-looking. Dressed in his dark attire, Heron stood there, graceful and noble, leaning up against the wall with a silly expression on his face. "Where do you think you are going?" he asked.

Cat's heart skipped a beat. "That's a pretty neat trick. I decided to go for a walk but sort of got lost."

Heron tilted her chin upwards with his fingertips. "It is delightful to wander, but never lose sight of where you started, or you will surely go astray."

Cat shook her head. Was this just practical advice, or did his comment have philosophical meaning?

"How did you know where I was?" she asked.

"You called on me."

"No, I didn't."

"Actually, you did." He gave her a playful look. "You mentally called out my name."

"I'm pretty sure I didn't, but I'm glad to see you anyway. I was afraid Brogan would be forced to call a search party."

"I understand your need to walk about and glad you had time to do so, but try not to fret about this evening." Heron stepped to the side, revealing Cat's chamber door.

"How... how did I get back here?"

Heron laughed. "You are a god, just like me. Control your environment by manifesting what you want, which in this case is your chamber door."

She smiled. "You manifested that, I didn't."

"Maybe I did," He winked and followed Cat into her room.

"What will you be wearing this evening?"

"Hmm, I don't know. Maybe the velvet lavender dress would be appropriate."

"Excellent choice."

She looked him up and down. "Seriously, Heron. How'd you find me? Is there a tracking device embedded in my skin somewhere?"

"I am a god. I can locate you anywhere."

Cat was intrigued. "That's reassuring. At one point I really thought I was lost." She strolled into the bathroom to prepare a bath.

Warm water streamed into the sunken bathtub. Catriona dumped a healthy portion of lavender-scented bath oil into it, inhaling deeply while the fresh aroma filled the room with its relaxing fragrance. She put it back on the side of the tub, then pulled her blonde hair into a loose bun.

Heron stood in the doorway, watching her intently.

"Can you turn around, please?" She started undressing.

"I have seen you in your naked glory. What is there to hide?" he said with a mischievous grin.

She noticed his deliciously wicked expression when the last piece of her clothing hit the floor. "If you continue to stare at me any longer, you might have to join me, and that would mean trouble."

"And that would be bad, how?"

"It wouldn't." She slipped into the heavenly water. "But I thought you said the Elders would find out."

"You are my responsibility, not theirs. As far as they are concerned, you are still wandering the hallways."

"How are you pulling that off?"

Heron knelt by the bathtub and swirled the water around her breast with his finger. "Pure magic."

Catriona's pulse quickened. "You're such a naughty immortal. It would be a shame to throw your nice clothes in a heap."

"I clean up fairly well." He stood up to undress.

Cat bit her lip. "Yes, you do."

A little over an hour passed before they emerged from her chamber. Cat was wearing a lovely lavender velvet dress with a scoop neck and tulle on the skirt. Her escort bowed and offered her his arm.

They walked down the corridors lined with white pillar candles casting their dreamy glow throughout the halls. The candlelight illuminated his magnificent immortal form. No one else was around, so she stole a quick kiss.

"What was that for?" he asked.

"I'm so glad you're with me."

"Are you not afraid someone will see?"

Cat shook her head. "No, I have yet to see anyone, which makes me wonder. Why is it I never pass one single person in these halls?"

He patted her hand. "You are our only guest."

"Why is that?"

"The Elder Temple provides guidance and a reprieve for souls to acclimate to the Thirteenth Realm when they first cross over."

They turned another corner and walked toward the entrance to the Temple.

"When the Questionings are going on, however, we must close it, allowing only the Observer to be housed here."

Cat looked around. "Well, it feels empty. Where do the other Elders stay?"

"We are anywhere we wish to be."

She frowned. "But your chamber is down the hall."

Heron shook his head. "That illusion was shown to you to provide comfort the first evening you were here. I do not actually need a chamber."

She stopped and stared at him.

"There is no reason for us to have our own chambers. We can be anywhere we want at any given moment and, believe me, there are marvelous opportunities for gods to explore in our vast existence. "

"How is it you appeared out of nowhere today?"

The Advisor chuckled. "I can change into anything I wish."

"Such as?"

"Any object... living or non-living. All forms of matter possess an energetic frequency and vibration immortals can adapt to."

Cat giggled. "So that's your secret. You can shapeshift?"

"Yes."

"You shift into other people and animals?"

"Yes."

"What about inanimate objects like a book, or a shoe?"

He chuckled again. "The gods created everything; therefore, we can become anything... even blend into walls."

"I see. I bet you were shape shifting your little self all over the place today watching me. Right?"

Heron gave her a devilish grin while opening the door.

"After you."

"Thank you, Sir," she replied.

As Cat and Heron ambled out of the Elder Temple into the streets, the entire Realm took on a carnival atmosphere. Colorful flags and banners darted up and down the torch-lit streets, while vendors swaggered about with their carts of food and novelties. The night was charged with excitement.

"This is amazing!" said Cat.

A young man offered her a white rose. "Are you the Observer?"

"I am." She smiled. "Thank you."

"They are happy to see you," Heron said.

The man took off running toward a bright, open area outlined by a wide hedge of tall trees.

"Where's he going?"

"The same place we are traveling to."

As they neared the large space, the people's yelling became louder, and multicolored lights zoomed over the treetops.

"Is this where the festivities are being held?"

Heron nodded.

When the pair entered the arena, the crowd shouted out her

name from all directions.

"Catriona! Catriona!" the people yelled, flocking around her.

She was a bit frightened but humbled by the outpouring of support. Up until that moment, Cat hadn't truly realized the importance of her role here. Most of her time in the Thirteenth Realm had been consumed with learning to overcome her weaknesses in preparation for what was to come. The magnitude of her mission hadn't dawned on her. For all intents and purposes, Catriona was the chosen one.

Heron escorted her up the stairs to the enormous stage, decorated in a three dimensional pattern with swatches of navy blue silk. Holes were punched through them to reveal silver lights resembling stars. In the middle of the stage stood a huge tree made out of silver metallic metal. The branches glistened with tiny white lights. The second Catriona's feet reached the stage; the lights flew off like a million rockets and burst in the air.

Catriona first spied Brogan and smiled, but the pit of her stomach lurched when she spotted Ruarc standing next to him. The Council Leader approached her and took her hand from Heron's to present her upon the stage. The people continued shouting until Brogan raised his other hand to quiet the crowd.

His booming, melodic voice addressed the large group. "May I introduce to you our lovely Observer, Ms. Catriona Blair!"

The crowd whooped and hollered for several seconds before being quieted down again.

"We are here in celebration of the Questioning. As most of you are aware, we had to postpone the festivities until she had recovered from her transition to the Thirteenth Realm."

Brogan turned to her. "Ms. Blair has already begun her portion of the Questioning with the Elders and will shortly be joining the Brotherhood."

The crowd cheered loudly.

As Catriona looked out into the audience, she noticed people who didn't wear bright colors signifying their professions. They wore white shirts just like Ruarc and the other Brotherhood members. Soon it was clear that they were from the Fortress of Shadows, here to partake in the celebration. How strange it was to see them standing with everyone else, and yet no one seemed bothered by it. Except for their clothing, there was no clear delineation between the two groups.

In Catriona's mind, black looked "evil." Ruarc wearing white and Brogan wearing black seemed backwards. If there was one thing Cat had learned, it was that nothing about the Thirteenth Realm matched her perceptions.

She glanced back at Ruarc. The sight of him made her tremble. She expected Heron to chime into her internal ramblings for encouragement, but then she remembered she must invite him in first by mentally calling out for him.

"Heron."

The Advisor ignored her. He just stood off to the side with a pleasant look on his face.

"Heron! I just wanted to invite you into my thoughts for protection."

"Understood," he responded.

The sound of his voice in her head brought about a much needed moment of relief.

Suddenly, Ruarc came up behind her and whispered in her ear. "You're a magnificent sight, Catriona. This shade of purple agrees with you."

"Thank you." She noticed his gaze lingering on her cleavage. Cat swallowed hard.

Brogan raised his arms. "And now, we invite all of you to enjoy the merriment!"

The crowd applauded.

Servers brought out a variety of gourmet foods on silver trays along with hundreds of golden chalices filled with wine. Everyone was being given a chalice to keep celebrating the event.

"Here is yours, my dear." Ruarc handed an emerald bejeweled cup to Catriona. "It goes well with your eyes."

She took it from him graciously, watching him partake of wine from his own chalice.

"I didn't think gods needed to drink."

"We don't, but I like the taste of wine... among other things." He had a glint in his eye.

Ruarc was dangerously charming. The medium length dark blonde hair, that he wore down for the evening, along with his striking jade eyes, would keep anyone entranced. She could see the threat he posed to her, but at the same time, he stirred her curiosity. His self-assurance, mixed with arrogance, made it easy for him to make his desires known. The leader of the Brotherhood was a beautiful immortal, but his sinister nature overshadowed everything.

"I should like to escort her around," Heron said.

"You've had this lovely creature's company," Ruarc replied. "Now I'd like to show her around for the remainder of twilight."

"Only part of the evening."

"Yes, Advisor," he said. "I promise I won't occupy her attention the whole night."

With that, Ruarc strutted past Heron with Cat, and they went down the stairs into the crowd, to fetch her something to eat. As they walked, he offered his arm. She knew she must play along and looped her arm through his, smiling.

Catriona let him lead her around, thinking she was a rabbit caught in his trap. This was reverse psychology, something she had practiced often in her counseling.

Ruarc grabbed a wooden skewer full of chunks of roasted chicken and vegetables from one of the silver trays.

"Here, you must be hungry," He held the food to her lips, trapping her arm under his.

She took a bite and chewed on the delicious tender meat before taking a sip of wine. "I am capable of feeding myself."

He offered her food again. "Let me treat you like a princess while you're in my presence."

Cat obliged, taking another bite. It was obvious he enjoyed making her dependent upon him by trying to hypnotize her with his sensuous behavior. It must be his form of control.

After she finished the skewer, Ruarc threw it on the ground. Then he walked her over to a tray of strawberries dipped in dark chocolate.

"You must try these, they are unbelievable."

He held the berry up for her, but before she could take a bite, he slid it seductively across her bottom lip. "Savor the chocolate first."

Catriona licked the sweet chocolate from her lip.

Ruarc smiled in approval and took a bite of the strawberry before offering it to her again.

This went on with each tray they sampled. At one point, he wiped food from her cheek and licked it with his finger. This uncomfortable exchange made her wish the night would be over quickly.

As the evening progressed, Cat's face warmed and flushed from all the wine. She looked down at her chalice, realizing it was always full. No one had been around to fill it, and yet it was filled to the brim.

"What is wrong?" Ruarc asked.

"It looks as if I haven't drunk any wine. How does my chalice keep refilling itself?"

Ruarc grinned. "I am taking care of all your needs."

She began to protest.

"Please don't be angry," Ruarc said in his husky tone. "I just want to make sure you're enjoying yourself. I only have your best interests at heart."

Cat's head started to spin. Stumbling slightly, Ruarc caught her and lifted her into his arms.

"Why don't we sit down?"

He set her down on a wooden bench nestled under some trees. Although she could see all the festivities around her, the area where they sat was further away and secluded. Cat didn't remember how they had gotten there so quickly.

Letting go of her arm, he took the chalice from her and set it on the ground. Then he reached for her hands again and held them tenderly in his.

"You just needed some fresh air."

Half of his face was in the shadows, and the moons were reflected in his dark pupils, giving the immortal a strange appearance. His intense mystical gaze bore into her.

"I want to get back to the festival." She looked around for anyone she recognized.

"I'll take you back, but rest, Catriona. I can tell you aren't feeling well."

Cat took in a few deep breaths.

"There, better?" he said. "I'd like to take this time for us to get to know each other."

"What is it you want to know?" She took another breath.

"About you, of course."

"Like what?"

Ruarc paused and rubbed his chin, giving Cat the opportunity to withdraw her hands from his clutch. "I suppose

I'd like to hear about your life on Earth."

His request seemed innocent enough, but he was throwing out easy questions. He was plying her with alcohol, hoping she'd have loose lips and would talk about anything.

"Tell me about yourself," he repeated.

Cat had to be wise with her words. "What do you want to know specifically?"

Ruarc casually sat back on the bench, crossing one leg over the other. "Everything."

She thought a moment. "I'm a counselor--."

"No," he interrupted, "I don't care about your profession. I want to hear about you. What are your likes and dislikes?"

Cat felt like a huge spotlight hung above her. Telling him all about her personal preferences made her vulnerable. The only thing to do was lie. Fabricating an image for self-preservation. Only people she trusted saw the real Catriona. If she claimed to like something, and didn't, he'd get a false sense of knowing her.

They sat talking for a long time. Cat only hoped she wasn't saying anything that could be used against her. Ruarc did all the listening, offering very little about himself. This immortal was slick in his interrogation, playing it in a non-intrusive manner. He was obviously trying to build a link of trust, but a sense of falseness lay behind it. He was looking for leverage.

Eventually the discussion had nowhere to turn but her family and profession. She couldn't deviate too much from the facts, since they had been monitoring her throughout her mortal life. Ruarc probed her with several questions, particularly ones about her family. Talking about them killed her on the inside, but she did her best to conceal her sadness.

"I can sense you miss them, but your mission will be short-lived," he said.

Cat walked a few paces away. The wine had made it hard to conceal her true feelings. She kept repeating Heron's words in her mind, knowing she'd never be able to see her family again.

Ruarc walked over to her. "Did I upset you?

"No... I think the wine has the better of me."

"Here, let me steady you."

Linking his arm with hers for support, he gently stroked the small of her back in a strangely soothing manner. "Better?"

Cat exhaled slowly, breaking away from him. "Yes, thank you."

He reached for her hand and kissed it.

"We will get the Questioning over as soon as possible."

She half smiled. "I'd like that."

"Let's sit back down."

"Oh, god... Heron. Where are you?"

Ruarc sat down and tapped the seat next to him. "Something has been puzzling me ever since you arrived in the Thirteenth Realm."

Cat feigned ignorance. "Really? What's that?"

"Heron is your Advisor? How did that happen?"

"I don't know."

Ruarc scratched his head. "Even an Observer has a final say in who their Guide will be prior to incarnating. I don't expect you to remember, but I find it curious that you chose an Elder. Did you choose him, or was it the other way around?"

"I'm sorry, Ruarc. I can't answer that... I really don't remember."

"Ah." He smiled. "But you do. You're hiding something from me."

"No, I'm not."

"You are. I can see it in those pretty ocean blue eyes of yours."

"Maybe he fancied me."

"Well, I can certainly understand why," he said, with a wicked grin.

Cat didn't respond. She wasn't savvy enough for a battle of wits with a god, not in her mortal state, and not half tipsy.

"I'm just fascinated," Ruarc said.

She needed to step up her game and downplay everything. "Honesty, Ruarc, I don't know what to say."

He smirked, realizing he'd get nothing more out of her. "I guess you don't. You both just seem comfortable with one another."

Cat's senses were on high alert. Had Ruarc or one of his minions seen them together?

"Well, Heron's been guiding me my entire life. Can't an immortal request to be a guide? At least that's what you said when you visited the Elder Temple."

"Immortals can, but I also mentioned how boring that would be. He's too protective of you."

Cat shrugged, but inside she felt like a derailing train. *"Heron, where are you?"*

Realizing she couldn't spar with Ruarc much longer, she turned the tables. "Don't tell me you're jealous?"

The menacing one frowned. "Jealous?" he scoffed. "Why would I be jealous?"

She smiled. "I'm teasing you."

He grabbed her hand and put it on his leg. "Gods are intrigued by their creations. I find it flattering that you're so interested in me." His seductive smile let her know she had opened a door that may not close. Sliding his arm around her, Ruarc whispered in her ear. "This conversation is getting boring. Why don't we think of something better to do?"

His lips brushed hers just before claiming them in a long, passionate kiss. Probing her mouth with his tongue, he caressed the side of her face and ran his hand through her long hair. She sighed, shocked at her own response. The intoxicating male scent of him made her melt in his arms. Why was her body betraying her? This was not what she wanted.

His hand slid under her dress, gently caressing an area that warmed under his sensual touch. She moaned.

Coming to her senses, she twisted her head to the side, pushing him away. "Get away from me!"

Ruarc smiled, breathing heavily. "You want more, I know it."

He leaned in toward her. Catriona wondered if she could handle another delicious assault.

A figure approached in the darkness.

"Your part of the evening is done, Ruarc," Heron barked.

Ruarc looked up and sighed. "Your timing is horrible, Advisor. Give us a moment longer, though, if you please."

Heron walked away from the bench but stayed close enough to monitor the situation.

Catriona stood up to leave and turned to say goodnight, but Ruarc pulled her back down. His face was inches from hers. "I will find out one way or another."

Stunned at his sudden change in disposition, she could only stare at him. How could he be so gentle one second and violent the next?

"Why are you being so cruel? We were having a lovely evening together, and now you want to ruin it?"

He grabbed her face. "You are delicious, Catriona. We will be spending more evenings together, I promise."

Ruarc gave her one last kiss before releasing her.

Cat stood and walked away.

Twenty-Two

Catriona brushed by Heron. For an instant, he stood dumbfounded; then he took strides to catch up with her. He grabbed Cat by the arm. "Slow down."

She pulled away from him and continued toward the square, thinking any moment she'd spiral to the ground from a wretched mixture of anger and distress. Never had the feeling of abandonment cut so deep.

He sprinted past her and halted Cat in her tracks, but she sidestepped him and kept walking. "Please stop and talk to me," he said.

Catriona went over to a secluded area and wrapped her arms around the trunk of a tree. It was the only thing she felt safe holding onto. Steadying her breathing, she tried to control her weeping, but the tears cascaded effortlessly down her face.

"I am sorry I did not come when you first called for me, but I had my reasons," Heron said.

She spun around in a rage. "They better be good ones!"

Heron looked around. He approached her and put his hands on her shoulders. "I needed to see his angle before I could help you."

Catriona couldn't speak. Her tear-filled eyes voiced her

despair. She put her head down.

Heron touched her cheek. "Ruarc deliberately plied you with alcohol, so you would say and do things you normally would not."

"You said you'd never let anything happen to me. You lied!"

"I am sorry." Heron sighed. "But I had to see how well you could conduct yourself without direct assistance."

Cat grabbed onto him for solace. "I was scared to death!"

"I know," he whispered, stroking her hair. "You do not understand the big picture. You will need to tolerate much from him, but I have faith in you. Have faith in yourself."

She shoved him away. "You have no right to patronize me! How the hell can you be all right with it?"

Heron's face twitched. "I have to accept what Ruarc does. Do not think for one second that it does not bother me."

"What do you mean you have to accept what he does?" she asked.

He grasped her back into a calming embrace. "Whether you understand this or not, there are many things you must endure. That is what I have been trying to prepare you for."

"You really can't help me all the time then, can you?"

"No, I cannot."

"But Brogan said I just needed to call out to you and you'd be there. Did he lie?"

"No, he didn't, but I cannot always be with you physically."

Cat looked up at him. "Oh, god. So, your 'assistance' will be nothing more than popping pleasant thoughts into my mind?" She let out a frenzied laugh. "This is just like the Stones. Once I get to the Fortress of Shadows, am I to assume I've got absolutely no control over anything, and neither do you?"

He shook his head, deflated.

"I can't do this."

"You must."

"I need you with me. Why can't you?"

"The energies in the Fortress are different. If I were to linger around all the time, without Ruarc's permission, it would make him more suspicious. And it is not what Guides do." Heron tightened his arms around her.

"I'm trapped."

"Shh," he said, wiping away her tears. "Come on, we should go back before anyone sees us."

The pair headed toward the square to join the rest of the festivities. They found Brogan and the Elders distracted by the frivolity around them. It was numbing to see everyone laughing and enjoying themselves even though Cat felt like she faced certain death.

"Come join me, Catriona!" Maeve shouted, with infectious enthusiasm. She grabbed her hand, pointing to the Ferris wheel.

Cat's mood lightened a bit when she spied the ride. With Ruarc parading her around, she'd had no time to marvel at the festive activity around her. The carnival atmosphere was charged with excitement. How could she stay upset when she spotted the games and all the rides she had yet to get on? Cat ran toward the Ferris wheel with Maeve and motioned for Heron to join them.

Heron had started running toward Cat when the Council Leader approached him.

"*Is she well?*" Brogan mentally beamed.

"*Ruarc is already conducting his part of the Questioning. He got her tipsy, tried seducing her, and then kept asking questions about our relationship. He will use whatever he finds relentlessly,*" Heron responded.

Brogan touched Heron's arm. *"You and I both understand why."* He inhaled sharply. *"I do not envy what she must go through under his care. At least she thinks she is merely mortal. That is one thing she has going for her."*

"Yes." Heron half smiled.

"Once she is done, you may tell her. For now, try to have some fun." Brogan walked away.

Heron took off toward the Ferris wheel. He spotted Cat through the crowd and waited in line for her. She appeared so childlike with that endearing smile. It warmed his heart. It was good to see her relaxed. Maeve must have used a bit of her own magic to help calm Catriona.

When an empty car came around, the three of them slid in beside one another and latched the bar across their laps. Up it climbed, rocking back and forth, moving slowly at first to allow others to get on. Once all the cars were filled, the ride went around nonstop. Cat had always loved the Ferris wheel. When she rounded the top, the crowd reminded her of little ants running around. Her favorite part, however, was looking up with the wind in her face, trying to peer into the heavens, pretending she could grab a star and hold onto it for safekeeping.

"I just love this ride," Catriona said. "I wish it would keep going…"

Just like that, her immortal wish came true. The ride went around and around, longer than normal. People were beginning to wonder if they'd ever get off. Most didn't complain, but a few grumbles were heard from the people below waiting their turn. It wasn't until Catriona decided she wanted off that the ride ended.

Back on the ground, Catriona spied a stand with cotton candy and caramel apples. "I thought they only served gourmet food here?" she asked.

"That was for your benefit, a celebration. Now they will serve all the treats you would usually find at a festival," Heron replied.

"Have some cotton candy with me, please?"

Heron cocked his head.

"Go on, Heron." Maeve said. "Eat some cotton candy. I will take a caramel apple."

They ordered a large bag of the sticky, puffy stuff. Cat opened it and grabbed a hunk. She made a yummy sound when it hit her tongue. This was comfort food. She tore off another piece and offered it to Heron, who only sniffed at it.

"Seriously, you'd pass up cotton candy?" She forcefully shoved it in his mouth.

Heron wrinkled his nose.

"Was that so bad?" Catriona giggled.

He licked the melted candy off his lips. "I never liked it, and still do not."

"I'm sorry," She wiped a spot of sugar from Heron's cheek. "Thanks for humoring me."

The threesome walked around a long time, chatting and admiring the festivities, until they came upon a ride called the Tunnel of Love.

"Last ride!" The operator yelled from his seat.

Maeve turned to them. "It appears the festival is ending. You both go enjoy yourselves while I go find Rhys."

Catriona seized her hand. "Thanks for joining us, Maeve."

Maeve smiled. "You are welcome."

Heron offered his arm while a sly grin spread across his chiseled face. "Will you accompany me?"

She smiled. "Why, of course."

They walked toward the ride's entrance, surprised there were no others in line before them. The operator acknowledged the couple, offering his hand to steady Catriona as she stepped into the tiny two-seater boat. It rocked in the water.

Her Advisor situated himself next to her. He looked over at the man and paused, glowering at him.

"What was that look for?" Cat asked.

"Nothing." Heron shook his head.

The operator gave them a mean grin. "Enjoy your ride."

They lurched forward into the dark passageway. For a moment, they were in complete darkness, but soon light burst through the tunnel, projecting hearts and flowers on the walls, while soft music played in the background.

"Romantic," Heron said.

Catriona thought about their previous encounter in the Blue Crystal Towers and her chambers. His nearness made her heart skip a beat. He put his arm around her and kissed her cheek. She welcomed his intrusion.

They drifted for a while, exploring the various passageways. A mist speckled Cat's cheek when they turned a corner. The music changed to a dramatic tone, and the lights blinked. She heard a roaring noise ahead and shrieked as water sprayed them when they plunged down a waterfall. Gusts of wind whipped around, tossing the boat in a simulated storm. Up ahead, waves of water splashed from the sides of the tunnel walls.

"Oh, boy!" Cat yelled.

"Hold on!" said Heron.

The boat pitched and turned. At first, it was all part of the fun, but soon it became much too turbulent. Waves of cold water splashed from all directions, drenching them, and Cat bruised her knee when it slammed against the side, nearly knocking her out of the boat.

Eventually, the turbulence stopped, and the waters became calm. The music and lights in the passageway faded. After drifting around in complete darkness for several seconds, Heron became alarmed.

"Something's not right," he said.

Cat called out. "Hello? Is anyone there?"

There was no answer.

She tried again. "Hello!"

Still no response.

At first, Catriona thought Heron had planned it this way, but after the night she'd already had, it seemed out of character to cause her any more alarm. Perhaps the ride had simply broken down.

A shadowy figure slowly took shape in front of them on a nearby platform. Catriona let out a sigh of relief. The operator! As they drifted closer, they recognized the figure standing before them.

"Isn't this cozy?" He waved his arms, and the lights came on.

Catriona panicked, recognizing the familiar voice. She squinted at the bright light surrounding them and held her hand over her eyes.

The menacing one stood smirking at them.

Heron held Cat, with one arm, in a protective gesture, looking at Ruarc in disgust. "That was you out there, was it not?"

Ruarc came closer and laughed. "Guilty as charged. I just wanted to check up on my favorite Observer."

Heron offered his hand to Catriona. He escorted her across an invisible bridge to the other side and turned to face Ruarc, his face only inches away. "You are toying with the wrong immortal!"

Ruarc grinned. "Am I?"

"Need I remind you of our history, or have you forgotten?"

Heron seethed.

"Our battles always turn nasty," Ruarc said. "But we're too equally matched."

"That has never kept us from leaving a path of destruction in our wake," Heron said.

"Stop it! Both of you," Cat said.

Ruarc turned to her. "She's right. We have to play nice or Source won't be pleased. I heard your cries and thought I could be of assistance."

Heron's eyes glowed like hot blue coals, piercing his adversary with his unwavering stare. "I never have needed, nor will I ever need your assistance."

The menacing one feigned innocence. "I'm only trying to help, but I see you're both just fine.

Heron bumped his shoulder against Ruarc. "Be careful, my friend." He pushed his way past him, and he and Cat walked away.

Ruarc stood still. "You, too… friend."

Heron's fingers dug into Cat's arm.

"Ouch!" she said.

He looked at her with his burning eyes. "I am sorry, but we must hurry back to the Elder Temple."

She stopped to gawk at him. *Never* had she seen Heron like this. His appearance was daunting, masking a rage deep within. Terror bubbled up in her throat. Cat was afraid of her beloved immortal.

"Never mind, just hold on!"

Heron lunged toward Cat and threw his arms around her. A sickening, whipping sensation, like her body falling backwards, was the last thing she remembered before opening her eyes to find them both standing in her chambers.

Twenty-Three

She glanced up at Heron, still in his grip. "How did we get here so fast?"

He appeared annoyed and released her. "Must you ask so many trivial questions?"

His bad temper made her tread lightly. "There's so much I don't understand about you. Sometimes you scare the hell out of me."

The immortal's eyes were back to normal. "There are things I will not be able to share with you, Catriona. I am not an open book for you to read. Until you are immortal again, there will be much about me you do not understand. It is a fact you will need to get over."

After the evening she had just experienced, Cat wasn't about to let Heron get condescending. "Yes, and you should remember I am mortal and won't pick up on all your nuances. That's a fact you'll need to get over."

Heron started for the door.

"Wait," Cat said. "Why are you taking your frustration with Ruarc out on me?"

Heron shot her a worried look. He came back and sat on the

edge of the bed.

Cat sat beside him, running her hands through his hair soothingly, and kissed him softly. Heron deepened their kiss and lifted her onto the bed.

"Whoa... wait a minute," she said.

Heron crouched over her, silent.

Her silence was a testament to her uncertainty about how to proceed with him, but Heron had no patience for it. He tilted Cat's chin up. "Speak words to me."

"What happened back there? Your eyes glowed... I've never seen you like that."

He said nothing, still looking at her with a serious expression. The awkwardness made Cat squirm under his weight. The immortal considered her a moment before rolling off onto his side.

Heron frowned. "I was angry, what is there to say? It is our nature."

"But why is Ruarc taunting you so much?" she asked, reaching for his hand.

Heron let out a deep sigh. "I cast him from this place."

"What do you mean?"

"I--along with a few other Elders--banished Ruarc from the Elder Temple."

"That must have been a long, long time ago."

"Yes."

"I thought you were a "young" god, if that makes sense. If you helped remove Ruarc, then you both must be ancient."

"In a manner of speaking, we are," Heron replied.

She moved onto her side. "Then tell me, am I also an old immortal?"

"No, you are not, and I do not want to talk about it."

Cat scooted closer and put her arms around Heron, wishing she could snuggle all the anger out, but he only pushed her away.

"Your feminine tactics will not work on me at the moment."

"But I'm only trying to comfort you."

"We both have had enough for the evening."

"Don't be angry with me," she said.

He turned to her. "I am not angry with you. I am angry with Ruarc. And I am frustrated about *all* of this." He opened the door. "Tomorrow, I will answer your questions, but for now, I must go."

Dejected, Catriona watched him leave. When the door latched shut, her heart burst in her chest. She buried herself under the comforter, and tears splashed on the pillow. The evening had left her nerves frayed, and she was so sick and tired of crying. *What will tomorrow bring?* Looking up at the ceiling, she went through the trials of the evening until exhaustion enveloped her in a slow, deliberate wave.

The dream had seemed so vivid. One minute she was creating objects out of thin air, and the next she was wielding energy balls and throwing them at formidable foes. She could smell the burning destruction around her. Brandishing power with such skill commanded respect for this intelligent, skillful, wise, compassionate, and creative immortal, Catriona. She had impressed herself and wanted to continue dreaming, but something kept tapping her on the shoulder.

"Wake up," a voice urged.

Catriona pried open her puffy eyelids, barely able to see. She sat up and noticed the horrific expression on Heron's face. She let out a small gasp at discovering the destruction around her.

"What happened?" she said.

"I should ask the same of you," replied Heron, putting out a small fire on the sofa. "What were you dreaming about?"

She paused. "I dreamt I was waving my hands around like I was creating something."

"Or destroying it." He opened his hand and the broken vase and Tiffany lamp, that lay shattered on the floor, floated off the ground. Within seconds they reassembled themselves, and they floated back where they belonged. Next, he waved his hands, and the rest of the mess instantaneously cleaned itself up as if nothing had ever happened.

Her mouth gaped open. "That's amazing."

He threw his arms around her and squeezed. "I should not have acted that way last night. It was not your fault." He rubbed her back. "I just needed time to wind down. I did not mean to upset you."

"I understand." She hugged him.

"You have been through a lot, and I need to be more sensitive. You asked me a question, and I am going to answer it even though it goes against my better judgment. I owe you that much."

"Why is it against your better judgment?"

"My dear, I have already gone against the wishes of the Elders... too many times to count."

She shook her head, "I don't want to get you in any trouble, Heron. If you're not able to tell me, then fine."

He smiled at her. "I am not ready to tell you many things, and yet I have. You asked if you were an old immortal. The answer is no."

"You already told me that."

"But what I did not tell you is that, although you are one of the youngest Elders, only the most powerful gods sit on the

Council."

"You're saying I'm a powerful immortal?"

"Yes, but do not let it go to your head," he teased. "I am actually next in line as the Council Leader after Brogan."

"You will be a great Council Leader."

"Thank you."

Cat wondered if it was safe to discuss the evening events. "How does Ruarc fit into all of this?"

"We were both original members of the Council. All was going as planned by Source, until Ruarc wanted more decision-making power for himself. At the time, humanity was not even in existence. We were working on other forms of creations on other planets."

"So what happened?"

"When the human project was implemented, Ruarc wanted humanity to go off in another direction, and he corrupted everything. You see, humankind was not meant to be in the state it is currently. Because of his intervention during the seeding process, the Elders are making adjustments as necessary."

"Ruarc was kicked out of the Council for being an asshole?"

Heron smirked. "He is one, but no. He was asked to leave by Source only after I, along with other Elders, gave a full report of our discoveries. He was punished fairly."

"He doesn't seem to see it that way."

"Ruarc views us as traitors, but he was the one who ruined everything. He was cast out, along with his followers, to the outer limits of the Thirteenth Realm."

"Is the Fortress of Shadows separate from the Thirteenth Realm?"

Heron shook his head. "There is only the magnificence of the Thirteenth Realm. Ruarc had to create the Fortress within it, in an effort to separate himself from the Elders. It is his own tacky creation, where he resides and takes souls that have lived a human life doing his bidding. They must go to the Fortress after death, for their kind is not welcomed here."

"Why didn't Source just stop him from having any more influence on humanity instead of allowing him to create the Fortress?"

"Part of humanity carries Ruarc's DNA. They are his lineage; he claims them."

His words confused her. "He fathered human children?"

Heron nodded.

"Did all the Elders?"

"Only those Elders who began the Council."

"Hmm... did you?"

Her Advisor bit his lip. "Yes, all of the original Council did. We are creator gods, Catriona. Sometimes we directly procreated, and other times it was done more scientifically. Why would you have an issue with it?"

"I don't. It's just strange to me."

He arched his brow. "Creation involves many working elements. It is part of evolution. Your immortal self already knows that."

"I suppose Ruarc's offspring don't play nice in the sandbox?"

"No, they do not, but we must allow them to interact."

She got out of bed and walked over to the food cart to get some juice. "Does Ruarc realize I am an Elder?"

"Of course not. You did not become one until long after he had been banished. And before you ask, no, you were not part of the human creation process. Only the ancient gods did that."

She winked at him. "What fun things did I want to create... seeding another planet, maybe?"

"Not quite," he replied.

"Then what is my great contribution besides agreeing to do all this?"

"Is not being an Observer enough?" he asked.

Cat swallowed her juice. "How do you know I'll make the right choice?"

"You are an immortal from the Council of Elders… it is who you are." Heron stood beside her. "You are our hope of gaining an advantage over the Brotherhood. That is why I am trying to protect and assist you every step of the way."

"Except you can't physically be with me all the time, so in essence I'm by myself."

"You will still feel my intrusion. I will guide you… just listen. You can do this, Catriona."

"Ruarc is gunning for you. He knows he can get to you through me. This is challenging for both of us."

Heron kissed her ear. "He cannot harm me, the two of us are evenly matched, but Ruarc can hurt you. I do not want to see that happen. His taunting is why I was so angry last night."

"And I can't use any of my powers?"

Heron sighed. "I performed that ritual in the Cathedral for several reasons, but knowing the ramifications of you regaining some of your powers," he pointed around the room, "my concern is you will be tempted to use them around Ruarc under extreme duress. You cannot let that happen."

She stroked his cheek. "I understand."

"I do not think you do," he warned. "I believe you will try not to use them, but you haven't considered what might happen if you do. Resist with all of your being."

"What happens after the Questioning… when I return to Earth?"

"Certain events will unfold after you have implemented the directives decided upon by both groups."

"Exactly what will I have to do?"

He dismissed the question. "Let us not discuss that just yet." He grabbed her hand and kissed her palm.

She wasn't satisfied. "Ruarc will see me walking through the streets of the Thirteenth Realm as an Elder, then what?"

Heron chuckled. "It will be too late for him to do anything about it."

"Bold plan," she said.

A devious grin spread over his lips. "I can think of a bolder one." Heron took the juice glass from her and laid it on the table. He scooped her up and gently laid her on top of the sage comforter.

"Oh, my. What kind of plan is this?"

"One where I believe the outcome is a win-win," he replied, crushing her lips with his.

Twenty-Four

It was déjà 'vu, sitting in the golden chair, looking up at the beautiful stained glass windows. According to her count, this was the fifth time she had sat in the Cathedral for questioning. Catriona pondered the discussions she'd had with Brogan and the Elders. The last time the Council Leader forced Cat into the Stones, she came back out explaining how it was a colossal waste of time.

None of them realized Catriona had a secret. She had made good use of her stay in the Stones to practice her divine gifts. She had discovered many, including her ability to be invisible and the power to see in the dark. It had been another exciting discovery.

Her powers allowed her to sense energy, even in darkness, so Cat had seized the opportunity to explore the void. It was a living organism, somewhat like a wormhole in space, and a big portal one could use to commute to other areas in the Thirteenth Realm. One time she had ended up in the Oval Room, and another time she had been in the Blue Crystal Towers... all undetected. It was a brazen move, but one she had to experience. With pure thought, the void took her wherever she wanted. The only snag was her inability to go to the Fortress of Shadows. Not that she relished going there, but Cat thought it would be wise to investigate the Fortress since that was the next phase of the Questioning. The void simply wouldn't take her there, making her wonder if the energy between the two dominions was not compatible, just as Heron had said.

"Are you ready?" Brogan asked her again.

"Huh?" She'd been daydreaming.

"Are you ready to conclude the Questioning?"

"Yes, I believe so."

Her Advisor sat behind her, his body language displaying how proud he was of the way she had carried herself throughout the process. Catriona seemed to have it all under control, and not once did he interrupt with thought transference. Most of her responses were quite thoughtful, yet indifferent, coming across as unengaged but truthful. This was exactly how she needed to be.

Brogan raised his arms for Heron and the other Elders to leave. They walked up the marble stairs of the Cathedral, one by one, and disappeared through the white doors. Brogan waited for the last Elder to exit before he followed.

Catriona wondered where they had gone. Maybe they had to vote to make sure everyone agreed she had passed. She waited patiently, tapping her fingers on the arm rest. While she sat there, itching to do something, she spied the prisms of light zipping around. They were quite entertaining once she stopped to look at them. Trails of light surrounded her like falling stars from the heavens. A few tiny beings came right up to Cat offering congratulations. She smiled, thanking them.

After a while, her legs became restless, and she kept crossing and uncrossing them. She was so bored, she eventually just stood up and walked around the Cathedral.

Brogan's voice chimed from behind her. "You are finished!"

She turned around, startled. "What? I... I am?" she asked.

"Yes, you may leave."

She raised her head and let out a breath of relief. She was so happy she almost threw herself to the floor in pure joy... it was over. Cat gleefully started back toward her chambers.

"No," he said.

"What?" She faced him.

He walked over and brushed a strand of golden hair from her eyes. "You are finished here at the Elder Temple."

"Yes, I understand that."

"Now you must leave."

Trepidation flooded her. "And go to my chamber?"

"To the Fortress of Shadows."

"But I need to say goodbye to Maeve and the others."

"There are no goodbyes. You will see them again," Brogan replied. There was a twinkle in his brown eyes.

"Can't I go back to my chamber and pack my things first?"

"No, sweet Catriona. There is nothing there for you to pack. Everything you need," he pointed to her heart, "is in here."

Catriona felt her head spinning. Was she ready to go to the Fortress?

Brogan took her hand. "It will be fine... come."

"Where is Heron?"

"He will be accompanying us in a while, but I am to escort you to the Fortress myself."

"How formal do we have to be?"

"Oh, there is nothing formal. I just need to make sure I personally deliver you to them. They are expecting you."

Catriona swallowed hard.

They walked outside into the glorious sunlight and took a winding path through the hills and mountains. The panoramic view was stunning, with the sunlight and vibrant colors, but not one bit of it seemed familiar. The path veered off toward the right. This was unfamiliar territory and an area Heron hadn't shown her.

A stream snaked parallel to the path. The sound of the running water was fluid and soothing. Serene wildflowers, in an array of colors, grew on the hillsides. Every once in a while, the breeze blew the flowery scent in Cat's direction. The grass was still just as lush and soft, prompting Cat to take off her shoes. She preferred going barefoot.

As they walked, Brogan continued holding her hand, patting it occasionally for comfort. He knew this part of her adventure intimidated her. Maybe that's why he chose to stay silent. Perhaps he felt that allowing Cat her time alone within her mind was best.

On and on they walked, up one hill and down another, until Cat wondered why Brogan didn't just transport them to the Fortress as Heron had done during the festival. But it occurred to her that their walking was part of the journey. Brogan wanted to give her space to reflect and prepare. For that, Catriona was grateful.

They reached the base of a mountain. "This is the last leg of our excursion," Brogan said.

She just looked up at its vastness.

Following him up the mountain, she breathed in the scent of fresh pine in the mountain air. The smell tickled her nose while she took in deep breaths of refreshing mountain air. The temperature was cooler and a light breeze blew, making the experience quite peaceful. Cat stopped a moment to sit on a large rock.

"Are you tired?" Brogan asked.

"No, not at all. I just want to take in the beauty."

He sat beside her. "You will be fine," he assured Cat in his melodic voice.

"I hope so."

"Do not worry. We will all be privy to your treatment at the Fortress."

"I didn't think the Elders and the Brotherhood exchanged information well," she commented.

"We do not, but we have our ways."

"Which reminds me," she said. "Heron has limited physical time with me in the Fortress of Shadows, so how will you know what's going on there?"

Brogan smiled at her. "We take many physical forms."

She looked at him. "What?"

"Shh," he said. "Let us just sit and listen."

They listened to the water coming down the mountain as it fed into the stream. The rushing water, along with the singing of a few birds perched on the trees above, soothed her. She looked up, realizing this was a pinnacle moment, symbolizing all she accomplished thus far. And even though she didn't relish the last half of her assignment, going to the Fortress of Shadows, she was grateful for the time she'd had with Brogan and the Elders.

After some time, the Council Leader turned and touched her shoulder. "We must continue."

As they hiked toward the top, the air got thicker and the delightful scent of pine, grass, and mountain air faded. Within a few paces, the path widened and the stream all but disappeared. When they reached the peak, Cat stared off into the distance, noticing that the valley below appeared faded. Its lackluster appearance gave it a pale look. Directly across from them was another mountain. On top of it, Cat spied the most enormous structure she'd ever seen. It expanded across the entire mountaintop and was surrounded by tall, thick walls. It certainly looked like a fortress.

"We are here," Brogan said. "You must continue on this path until you get to the wall. Once you are there, announce who you are, and they will let you in."

Catriona gave him a kiss on the cheek. "Thank you. I won't let you down." Her voice wavered a bit, but Cat was not about to appear weak, not now.

"Dear Catriona. It is not me you need to worry about disappointing. It is mankind."

She chuckled nervously. "No pressure then, right?"

"Heron is waiting for you at the wall," he bellowed to her as he made his way back.

She watched him leave, turning around for only a split second to look at the fortress. She turned around again to say something to Brogan, but he had vanished. She felt deflated. Cat spun around to head toward her morbid destiny.

As she crossed the valley, it seemed like the path went on forever, yet she wasn't tired despite the stale air. It had a strange aroma, with no scent of flowers or trees. She was surrounded by nature, but it was not as bright and vibrant. The only comparison she could think of between the two dominions was that one took on the hue of a deep oil painting and the other was in watercolor.

Once she started up the second mountain, the scenery changed. The air was getting heavier, and the closer she came to the Fortress, the more menacing it appeared. It was an entire city surrounded by thick grayish stone and concrete. It was Medieval in appearance, with tall bartizans and arrow loops in the walls. The main entrance was an enormous Barbican structure with a portcullis that a cruise ship could fit through. She could just make out enormous spires sticking out the top of a building that sat further beyond the entrance. The building looked almost like a temple, but not quite. All Cat knew was that despite the differences between the two realms, the Fortress drew her toward it in a mystical, seductive kind of way.

The lighting was odd. Although the sun was shining, something in the air diffused the light. It wasn't thick like fog, but a thin layer of mist gave off a muted orange glow, distorting the light, giving it a dreamy look. The mist made everything dull and depressing. Nothing was pristine.

When Cat reached the entrance, she looked up at the intimidating Fortress. She peered through the gate. People bustled around inside. They were dressed in white shirts and dark pants or skirts. Everyone looked the same, unlike the people in the other part of the Realm. Cat wondered why their clothing didn't signify a professional designation, as they appeared to be scurrying off to work. An energy field encircled these people and buildings, too, but it didn't have the same brilliance as the other side of the Thirteenth Realm.

She stood and wondered who would let her in. A metal cranking sound startled her. The portcullis rattled as the massive metal gate went upward in slow motion. Cat froze, staring at it in awe. When it stopped, she reluctantly entered, surveying the area. She wandered around, expecting to see Heron waiting for her, but he was nowhere to be found. Where could he be? Cat was completely lost. The people acknowledged her, but no one smiled. A frantic feeling crept up in her throat. This certainly was not the atmosphere she was used to. Cat went further into the structure and found the enormous spires she had noticed from the mountain. She was drawn toward this building by what felt like a magnetic pull. It was made of gray stone and resembled a medieval church with tall spires and a huge bell on top. The gigantic building sort of resembled a temple, but much more extravagant and gaudy.

"Catriona!" a voice boomed from behind her.

Cat spun around to find a warm smile and sparkling green eyes staring back at her. Ruarc had on the same white button-down shirt, with rolled-up sleeves, and black pants. His smile turned into a sensual grin, while his demeanor shifted to exhibit his propensity towards arrogance. He grabbed her hand, and he nudged her forward, through the streets, toward the massive building. It was obvious he'd been expecting her.

"Welcome, dear Catriona." He waved his free hand around.

"Welcome to the Fortress of Shadows."

#